C'mon And Do The Apocalypse

Volume One

C'mon And Do the Apocalypse: Volume One
28 Days Of Mutilated Zombie Whores Later
My Wife Dawn…And The Dead
Published by Zelmer Pulp Press
The Copyright belongs to Ryan Sayles & Brian Panowich
2012.
All Rights reserved.

Cover Design by C D Regan

Zombie photos by Lee Hartnup

The authors worked extremely hard to bring you this work
of fiction so please don't steal their shit.

Amazon first edition 2012

For Donna

For Dawn

C'mon And Do The Apocalypse

Volume One

Featuring:

A word of Introduction
By Ryan Sayles

*

The prequels

*

My Wife Dawn…And The Dead
By Brian Panowich

*

28 Days Of Mutilated Zombie Whores Later
By Ryan Sayles

Crime has been good to me.

Made a lot of friends. A little bit of money. People whom I don't know, know me. That might be bad for some folks, but for a crime author it's what you need.

And one of the friends I made was a dude from down south by the name of Brian Panowich. We've been published on several of the same crime fiction sites and eventually became friends the 21st Century way: on Facebook. So you know it's legit. (on a separate note, Brian says he only uses FB for his writing contacts, networking, et cetera but I see he's made friends with all the gay porn stars he could find as well as Sesame Street, so…)

But anyways, I was getting jittery. I had a book out (*The Subtle Art of Brutality* put out by Snubnose Press, and yes, it is available in eBook and paperback on Amazon and B&N, thank you for asking) and a column on *Out of the Gutter*, but all sorts of collections and anthologies and cool stuff were popping up without me being in them. You can see how that hurts my ego.

I got tired of things going on that didn't involve Ryan, so I started looking at my options. And that was about the time I read an interview with Brian where he said he'd love to write a story about the zombie apocalypse. Bingo. Huge audience? Check. Endless possibilities? Check. Drowning in cash money after we deposit the first royalty payment? Check. Errr…. Well, not so much, but still.

So we made a plan to release a split. Brian had networked with everybody under the sun, and one of those people was a writer/artist by the name of Chuck Regan. Chuck did the cover for us. Somewhere down the line, among everything else, Chuck decided it needed an imprint badge in the corner like all the old school pulp books used to have.

We named it Zelmer Pulp. Zelmer is a family name for me and I gave it to my oldest son. Brian, wishing he had my babies, suggested the idea and of course I went with it. You can see how that strokes my ego.

We released the split and out of nowhere two dudes pimped it like it was their own project. Isaac Kirkman and Chris Leek, two other great guys who also happen to be great crime writers. About the time those guys were shoving copies of our zombie split down the throats of the general public, Brian came up with the idea to do another Zelmer Pulp issue, but make it science fiction this time. It just so happens that Chuck is a sci fi author.

Isaac and Chris worked this thing for cash and prizes and we knew we had to have them on board. Why not reward them for their hard work by allowing them to claim me as a friend and writing partner? Seriously. There's no greater honor. We all sat down around the campfire (metaphorically) and formed a band (also a metaphor). But we were missing one thing. Just one thing we couldn't do without. An asshole.

Enter Rich "Nora Roberts" Osburn. Him, his skinny jeans, extensive tattoo work and even more extensive collection of custom-made Lederhosen completed us (not metaphorical).

We were Zelmer Pulp.

Aquaman jokes, a Twitter account and endless BS postings in our private FB chatroom. Isaac being endlessly supportive of everything, Chris taking entire days off because his irritable bowels won't allow him the time to type without clenching up and causing too many misspellings. Rich and Brian going back and forth in endless (and moronic) insult-laden tirades. Brian getting drunk and posting "yo mama" jokes written in Ebonics. Chuck bragging about all the success he has in his other ventures and how we're all poor and white trash. Me, sobbing about how often my wife is pregnant, but how it's never my kid.

It's a boy's club. And, we write some damn good stuff.

So enjoy Brian and I's foundation here. The next issue, coming soon to an Internet near you, will feature the whole crew as we rip Sci Fi a new one. Maybe giggle and slather on some KY while we do it. I don't know yet. Hell, we might not need it. Then? More zombies. Then? Whatever we want.

Because while our respective wives browbeat us and make us wear women's' panties while we cry and scrub the toilets, in Zelmer Pulp we answer to no one. You hear me, God? NO ONE!

Just kidding God. Please don't strike us down. Not now. Not while we're doing so well. Please.

Well, maybe Brian. But not me.

Thank you.

Ryan Sayles

Kansas City, Missouri

2013

Prequel One: The Code

Static.

"Gold Cross Unit 26, respond to a seizure at forty four Newbury Ct."

Static.

"That's us Phillip, let's go."

" 26, be advised the patient is a juvenile. Respond on EMS tac one."

"Step it up Phil, it's a kid."

Andre flipped on the emergency lights and siren, and grabbed the radio.

"26 responding."

Phillip pulled a U-turn across the four-lane highway, pushing the ambulance toward their latest call. The evening had started out slow, but over the last few hours, every available box in the street was in route to something. Looks like it was going to be one of those nights.

"Newbury is right off Pepperidge, we should be there in no time."

Phillip nodded and weaved the truck through the traffic.

Andre grabbed the radio again when they arrived at the residence.

"Dispatch, 26 is on the scene, forty four Newbury Court."

The two Paramedics were barely out of the truck before the front door of the residence burst open. A tall shaggy headed young man carrying a smaller kid met them in the yard.

"He just started freaking out. I can't snap him out of it."

"Calm down sir," Andre said, "Can you tell me some history on him? Does he have any medical conditions?"

"No, man, nothing. I don't know what's happening."

"What's his name?"

"Bobby."

How old is he?"

"Fifteen."

Andre pulled out his penlight and shined it into the boy's eyes, lifting his eyelids to see his pupils.

"Damn, he's burning up. How long has he had this fever?"

"I don't know." The older kid said. "I came home and found him laying on the floor like this."

"How long ago?"

"Maybe ten minutes ago. I called 911 as soon as I found him."

Andre motioned to Phillip to get the stretcher, and took the boy from the young man.

"Is the mother here?"

"No. She comes and goes. I'm his brother, we kind of just take care of each other."

"Well, listen to me. Your brother's fever is life threatening and we're going to take him to the hospital, do you have a way to reach your Mom?"

"What's wrong with him." The older boy was starting to lose it. Tears were beginning to well up in the corners of his eyes.

"Does your brother do any drugs?"

"What? no. Hell no! He's a good kid."

"I have to ask. At this point it could be anything, but we need to get him to the ER as soon as possible."

Andre and Phillip loaded Bobby's shivering lanky frame onto the stretcher and packed him into the back of the ambulance.

"I'll run a line on him and hook up the monitor." Phillip said.

"No, I got it. You just get us to University. High flow diesel."

Phillip acknowledged and hopped behind the wheel. Andre turned back to Bobby's brother who was staring through the open back door of the ambulance in horror.

"We got him." Andre said. "You can follow us to University, but don't speed. And call your mother." With that, he slammed the door and Med Unit 26 headed out with a fury.

***

"Dammit, I can't hold him still enough to get a stick. I'm going to have to restrain him."

"Be careful back there 'Dre, you don't know what that kid is on."

"I can handle it, just haul ass. This poor kid is circling the drain."

The kid was on fire and the convulsions were getting worse. Andre was struggling to get him restrained when the boy slacked and went still. Andre looked at the monitor with the familiar dread every Paramedic knows all too well.

"Fuck me, Phillip he's flat-lining! Goddamn it, how far out are we?"

"Five minute ETA."

Andre put two fingers on Bobby's still throat. Nothing. No Pulse. He put his ear to the boy's bluing lips. Nothing.

"Shit, shit, shit, shit, shit, shit,"

Andre straddled the boy and started compressions. Pushing hard and deep while trying to keep his balance in the speeding ambulance.

"Get on the horn, Phillip, let them know we're coming in hot."

Phillip grabbed the radio.

"Med 26 to university."

Static.

"Go ahead 26."

"We've got a full code coming to you. Fifteen-year-old male. CPR in progress. Two minute ETA."

"Received 26, we'll have a team in place."

"Holy shit, Phillip!" Andre yelled. "I got him back! Brother, I got him back!"

Bobby was starting to stir underneath Andre and the movement washed the Paramedic with relief. This kid wasn't going to die on his watch. He reached down to the boy's jugular to feel for a pulse but Bobby's head twisted back and forth making it impossible.

"Is he stable?" Phillip yelled back.

"Hell yeah! I can barely keep him on the stretcher."

"What are his vitals? I'll radio ahead."

"I don't know. The monitor must be broken. It's still showing a flat line."

"Well fuck it, we're here."

Phillip wheeled the ambulance up the tarmac and a team of Nurses popped open the back doors. They unloaded the writhing, growling teen and rushed him inside. One of the Doctors looked confused.

"I thought you said this was a code?"

"It was." Andre said. "We got him back."

"I would say so." The doctor said watching the group of nurses and orderly's struggle to keep the boy restrained.

***

Phillip finished his verbal report to the counter nurse with the little bit of information they had on the kid, stripped the sheets off the stretcher, and wheeled it back outside to the truck. Andre was sitting on the bumper.

"Good job back there man. You saved a life today."

"Yeah, I guess so."

"Hey man, are you alright? You look like shit."

"All of a sudden I feel like shit too. And look at this."

Andre lifted his arm to show his partner a small wound on the underside of his left bicep.

"I think that fucker bit me."

***

Prequel Two: Room 7 Slaughterfest

"They should have taken this one to Research hospital," Jo Ann says, clutching at the kid's left arm.

I grapple with the right arm, find his nails clawing at me. "Or left him in the damn street where he could OD in peace."

We rush from the ambulance bay down the long, tiled hallway and around the corner. Enter into the ER proper. Halls of rooms unfold before us, everyone diddling about in their own small worlds as Rick treats room 3 and Diance treats room 20 and Doctor Cline consults with Beverly about room 14.

We're packed to the gills tonight.

"Room 7, guys." Kate, the nurse, rushing alongside. Genuinely concerned for this drug addict. Gotta be a fiend. PCP. Bath salts. Meth. Whatever. EMS said in report he never used, but the one thing you can count on as truth is: people lie.

Room 7. We duck in, techs waiting for us with restraints. The kid is flailing, jaws flexing aimlessly like the very air he breathes is tar-like. His eyes dead yet possessed. Doper.

We're shorthanded tonight. The triage waiting room is full. Joan Ann and I are the only armed security in the place, spending all of our time doing orderly work in the Emergency Room. Sitting on jackass punks who get a bad trip and decide they need professional help to nurse themselves through their own mistakes.

Kate looks to Doctor Behn standing in the door. "Can we get some Ativan and Haldol?"

The doctor ruminates like an educated boob, turning over the drug question like it were some perplexing philosophical answer to the existence of God. Meanwhile we're wearing down, struggling against this kid, and he's not even breathing hard. He's burning up, though.

"Do we have a name? History?" Doc asks, hands in pockets.

"We got something at report."

Finally, "Well, go ahead. One mil of each. But add one of Benadryl in there also."

Lauren, another nurse, takes off to that magic Never-Never Land where the heavy drugs are kept.

The kid's feet get restrained. Jo Anne Puts her body weight on the kid's arm. He's a machine. Moans, nothing more. Kate tries to talk to him but he's too far gone. Thousand yard stare. But he's aggressive. We gotta watch it.

I have my territory. His right arm. I hold it. Look over at Jo Anne, see her exhausted. We've wrestled two people her tonight already. Psych patient who smelled like BO and bathtub scum and some homeless guy who was using the ER as his personal toilet.

Now this junkie kid.

"Get Jo Anne's arm next," I say, bead of sweat running into my eye. Burns. I hate that kind of sting. Feels corrosive almost. And this was a *big* bead. Without thinking I lift one hand up, take off my glasses to wipe my eye.

Flash of struggle. Kid's arm is free. I get thrown off balance as he makes his move. I step back, foot lands on the leg of some blood cuff stand. Nearly fall. Jo Anne screams. Kate screams. Lauren, suddenly in the door of the room, screams. On my feet. Jo Anne, pulled across the kid's chest. So strong. She's gurgling now. I see wet red. I smell copper. Blossom of crimson, spreading. Alive almost. Surreal. I need to be somewhere else. Somewhere warm and tropical and full of sandy beaches, lazy breezes, not a sterile hospital room filled with buzzing fluorescent light and shrieking women. The kid is chewing on my partner's neck. Blank mind. I know my hand goes to my sidearm. I lurch forward, stab the barrel into the kid's ear. Pop, pop. Brains paint the wall, Kate covers her mouth, stifles her screams.

I lean back, finger still squeezing the trigger from that last discharge. "I had to I had to I had to I had to I had to I had to I had to I had to-"

Nobody moves. The kid, slack. The side of his head facing me, just two small holes. The side facing away, gotta be a gaping void. An empty, gaping void. Lauren, in shock and must be numb, she takes a step forward. Kate is looking at Jo Anne. They both reach for her, as she slumps over the body of the kid. Her own blood soaking the kid's clothes.

And, some kind of black stuff. Like foam. Dyed foam.

Kate and Lauren go her side and I holster. Step out of the room. See the entire ER has paused in their own sufferings, their own pains and illnesses and left the comfort of their own rooms to stand in the hallway and gawk and whatever is going on in room 7. I take a deep breath, can't get any air. Shirt is too tight. The hallway is squeezing. All the sounds in my ears—the ones that make it around the high-pitched note left behind by the gun shots—are all slurred. Lights filter through my eyes wrong; picking out the harsh cast and making them worse. Like twin suns glaring into my pupils. I can't handle this.

I just killed a kid. I just killed a kid who killed my partner. I just wiped a bead of sweat away and because of that, I gave him the hard goodbye. A kid. A doper, a cannibal. But still. Holy shit. I'm going to get fired. The city is going to have to investigate this as a homicide. Hopefully the DA rules it justified. Civil court. I wonder if the kid's parents are the suing type. The hospital is going to pour over me, the media will know in minutes I'm sure-

More screaming. Terrible wailing.

I turn around, peer back into the room. I don't even really notice the gun is back out now. Lauren stumbles back, falls. Her forearm missing a chunk. Kate slumps into a corner, one hand limply holding back a gout of blood spurting from her neck. Her face knows what her body is finding out: she's dead.

And there is Jo Anne, standing upright, face covered in slick blood as her mouth burbles over with a black foam. Her eyes dead and yet possessed, snarling like an animal. Kate is smeared in that black foam. Lauren is smeared in that black foam.

Jo Anne growls and walks towards me. I pump four rounds into her white polo shirt. Shatter her name tag, the force of the hits making her cross necklace flop around on her chest. Nothing. Jo Anne doesn't even flinch.

I empty the weapon. She doesn't even really bleed. Just keeps coming. Paralyzed. I can't think. My mind wanders off to that warm, tropical place as Jo Anne's hands reach for me. But what I really see is Kate.   She stands back up. Black foam cascading from her mouth.

The ER is so full tonight. My God we are packed to the gills.

***

MY WIFE DAWN...AND THE DEAD

By Brian Panowich

December 22, 2012

The night the world went down the shitter, just so happened to coincide with my wife's third annual Christmas party. That turned out to be piss poor luck for me, because I knew I was going to catch a lot of grief about it. Don't get me wrong, I'm not trying to downplay the apocalypse, but from the inception of my marriage I've been seeing my girl through all kinds of *end of the world* scenarios, botched job interviews, no-show babysitters, etc. Once I was convinced the end was near over a misunderstanding about what to eat at *The Olive Garden,* so I found it strangely ironic that this crisis about to ruin my wife's intricately planned get-together actually *was* the end of the world.

Amongst her many talents and abilities, my wife Dawn is a consummate decorator, almost to a fault. The girl loves her holidays. Lavish red and green sparkling knickknacks, and a vast collection of nutcrackers, were all over the small townhouse we shared with our four children. Gone were the pumpkins and candy corn scented air fresheners of Halloween. Gone were the harvest browns and gold's of Thanksgiving. On December one, they were rapidly replaced by pine wreaths and stuffed snowmen, harbingers of the winter solstice ahead. Tonight, Fresh-made varieties of Chex mix, she labored on until the wee hours the night prior, were all arranged in their sparkling dishes on the dining room table. Cheese and veggie trays formed an edible wagon train looping around the poinsettia centerpiece she had custom made just for this occasion. The girl always has a plan, a better plan, a vision, and to deviate from that vision is to invite chaos to rain down on your life and I'm good with that. To me she is every bit like Haley's Comet. A woman of her caliber only comes around once in a lifetime. And where as most people just look up to the sky and say *wow*, never really understanding what they are looking at, I get it, and intend to hold on with both hands. For better or worse, because believe me, there's way more better than worse.

My humble addition to the evenings spread was an ugly stainless steel crock-pot full of my world-renowned firehouse chili. Our friends love it, so she allowed it to be served, but it had been exiled to the far end of the kitchenette bar so not to be seen mingling with the high-end serving dishes. This ugly chili pot is where the fellas and me would congregate later with stiff bourbon cocktails and lies, while my woman played hostess to the other wives. She'll show off the kids handmade stockings hanging by the chimney with care, and the fresh cut mistletoe above the back door. I'll watch her work the room and remember why I married her. She shined. I mean, really shined. She glowed with a soft sparkle when she was in her element. It made everyone around her look grey in comparison. She was an absolute joy to be around during one of these soirees. It was getting past the sheer terror of Dawn in *Preparation-to-shine* mode that was so daunting. A few good men have tried and failed, but of course, they aren't me.

We have four children between us, a little hers, mine, and ours. It's always a revolving door of kids around our house as they each take turns spending the weekend with their respective other parents. That's normally where they would be on a night like tonight, but in a moment of haste we decided to let our three youngest kids, including our baby boy Wyatt, spend a few days at my father-in-law's place. Dawn's Dad lived by a pond on a huge chunk of property up in North Georgia, and now that the babies were all potty trained, Papa Ed had been more receptive to overnight visits. The kids loved it there, and they loved him, so three problems solved. That left my oldest daughter, and the source of Dawn and I's first pre-party spat.

"Are you kidding me?" she said, waving her spatula at me. "I have spent a small fortune on this party, from the food, to the decorations, to the that ridiculous *Knob Creek* you insisted we have for your good buddy Eric, and now you want to throw a nine year-old into the mix? Really?"

"Baby, she just turned ten."

"Nine, Ten, she's still a child! Once, maybe twice a year, we get to be adults, we get to be around other adults, and you want to ruin that."

"I don't want to ruin anything. We promised her last year when she turned double digits we would consider letting her do stuff like this. She doesn't want to hang out with the little ones. She's getting to the that age where she wants to do more grown up things."

"But she's not a grown-up, she's ten, with no business being at an adult Christmas party."

"I promised her."

"You promised me!"

"What did I promise you?"

She shot me the look that implies I never listen to anything she says. It makes my face burn.

"You promised me I could have this. One night to relax and feel like a normal person and not a mother of four."

"And you can still do that. Nothing changes."

"Are you serious? Everything changes. You know as well as I do, we can't be ourselves with the kids around."

"Not *kids*, just Talia."

"It might as well be all of them. Your daughter is the hardest to control."

There it is. She only calls her *my daughter* when I am dangerously close to losing any chance of ending this peacefully. I needed to concede and let her have this. Kiss her on the forehead and tell her *of course baby, whatever you want*. Instead I say:

"Goddamn it Dawn, I want her here."

"Watch your mouth!"

Nothing makes the space between my eyes burst with the fury of a thousand exploding suns like when my wife tells me to watch my mouth. I'm turning 41 this year. I feel like I've earned the right to say whatever I want in my own house. She can see I'm fixing to spout all that nonsense out when she points the brownie batter covered spatula at the hall behind me.

"What's going on?" Talia said.

I think being told to curb my fowl mouth stings so much because deep down I know she is one hundred percent right. She's always right, and I'm an Idiot.

"Nothing Baby, Here..." Dawn handed the spatula to *my daughter* and Talia trotted off into the living room to admire the gifts under the tree. Expertly wrapped gifts.

"Sorry Baby." I said, sounding like *I* was the ten year old in the room.

"She can stay, but if I end up wrangling her all night. You are *NOT* getting lucky tonight."

"Thank you."

'*Your welcome*' was implied by her silence; at least that's what I chose to believe. She grabbed another spatula, and I ceased to exist.

***

I guess it all started with Dave. I'm not saying it was his fault, but Dave finally showing up was when everything started to go south. He was late. Dave was always late. He was my best friend, but ever since I'd known the guy, he couldn't show up on time for anything. He always had a good excuse though. Tonight it was the snow. It was only about three inches of powder that most likely wouldn't stick around till morning, but the slightest hint of snow in Augusta Georgia could shut the whole town down. Nobody knew how to act. Everyone battened down the hatches like it was the end of the world. Dave brought his youngest daughter, Jazz, who was a product of a wildly unsuccessful five-year marriage. Dave wasn't the marrying kind, but he *was* the fathering kind. His 17 year-old stepdaughter Ashley, and the gloomy introverted 15 year-old Jazz, were a pair of beautiful, thoughtful kids. The kind you hope your own kid's turn out to be.

"No Ashley tonight?" I asked as he shook off the snow in the foyer and helped Jazz out of her parka.

"Nah, she's got a new boyfriend, so hanging out with Dad is not cool any more. She said she would stop by later if she had time."

"See baby," I tuned to Dawn, "Dave brought *his* daughter." She ignored me and went on showing Diane and Tilmon, who had been the first to arrive, the never-ending stream of family photos on her iPhone.

"Come in and get comfortable," I said, turning back to Dave, "I'll make you a drink." I knew he would want a beer instead of bourbon, a Guinness stout to be exact. He had been drinking that swill since we were kids. He was late all the time, had terrible taste in beer, and his stories went on a little long, but he was the first friend I made when my old man moved us to Georgia and the first friend I really considered family. He was also the first one of us to die.

***

David and Jazz showing up completed the guest list. At least of the guests we expected to show up. We always put invitations out to work friends at the firehouse and Dawn's office, but never counted on seeing them. Diane and her new husband Tilmon were the first to arrive. Eric and his wife, Stefanie, got there shortly after, looking fresh out of an argument of their own that lasted all the way up to our front door. Eric and Tilmon were drinkers, so they were already on their second hefty dose of *Knob Creek*, huddled around the chili bowl. The girls were tipping back glasses of red wine and *Bing Crosby* sang on the stereo. Jazz had settled into the corner of our plush red sofa with her ever-present e-reader. Over the last year, Jazz had developed a new Goth persona, complete with black fingernails, dark clothes, and every vampire romance novel under the sun. Every kid goes dark for a while when they hit the teenage years, and now it was Jazz' turn. Talia was as close to her as possible without being conjoined. The smiles were genuine. These people warming up my house were the home team. The friends with kids that rarely got out, and honestly enjoyed each other. With Dave finally there, it felt like we could stop waiting and relax. It felt like Christmas. For a brief moment I was in awe of my wife and the way she could single-handedly craft a memory. She floated around the room, filling glasses and being perfect, and every now and then she would give me the look. The look she gave me when I first saw her on a bar stool at Club 1102. The same look she's giving me in the 11x19-wedding photo above the dining room table. The look that melts me down to the wick, and makes me believe that maybe---just maybe---God exists. If he did though, apparently he didn't want me staring at his handy-work that night because that's when he turned out the lights.

***

We lost power a little after 9 PM. The sudden darkness and abrupt halt of *A Bing Crosby Christmas* was jarring.

"Boom, boom, out go the lights." Eric sang with a drunken sailor slur.

I made my way to the pantry to find a flashlight. I can't say I was completely surprised. The underground power to this section of town must have been installed half-assed. They never held up to anything. A strong gust of wind could knock our power out, so during thunderstorms we almost expected it. We stayed prepared with tons of candles and Flashlights. I bought flashlights, Dawn bought candles---lots of candles. The snowstorm outside started out as a complement to the evening, but had just graduated to my wife's shitlist.

"Daddy, the lights went out."

"I can see that T, just stay on the couch, and I'll bring you a flashlight."

Dawn met me in the kitchen and pulled out the stash of candles.

"Well, this sucks." she said.

"Yeah, hopefully it'll be back on shortly."

"The candles will make everything look cozy." She said. She had a wine buzz. It made her even sexier.

"I like it when you get a buzz"

"Well, you're not out of the doghouse yet mister, so go see if the power's out all over. I got this."

"You sure?"

"I got this." She repeated and kiss-pushed me out of her way. I watched her walk away and started toward the door.

Come to think of it. It was loud outside. Then sudden silence in the house made all the yelling outside much more apparent.

"I'll come with you, man." Tilmon said. Tilmon was a big boy, and I guess he thought I needed the back up if a troop of neighborhood kids slinging snowballs assaulted me.

"Me too." Eric chimed in.

"Um, no." His wife chimed back, "Your not leaving me here in the dark."

Eric stopped chiming.

He was that guy. I don't want to say he's simple, but he is the kind of guy that is mostly oblivious to the world around him all for the reward of a beer and smoke at the end of the day. The truth is, I envy him.

I opened up the front door and saw the snow was thicker than I expected. It looked like we might get an honest-to-God snow day the next morning. It made me regret the kids not being here, but glad Talia stayed. Maybe I could get a little daddy-daughter time tomorrow. The powder was coming down pretty steady, and the only light anywhere was coming from the moon. The moon was huge. I remember that. A lot of people were outside looking up at the sky and a few kids were wrestling in the snow a few yards over. I think they were wrestling. There was a lot of yelling too. I know we rarely get weather like this, but still, it was after nine at night. No need for all the yelling.

"It looks like a silent night" my neighbor Chris yelled to me over the racket up the street and I wondered if he got the irony of that. He was holding his eight-year-old daughter Isabel who was wrapped up tight in a puffy hot pink snowsuit.

Who has snowsuits on hand in this town? I thought.

"We got plenty of candles if you need anything," I yelled back. "Booze too."

"Thanks man, the wife is down with a nasty cold, but maybe I'll stop by later. Right now I think I'm gonna build me a snowman with the kiddo."

"You know your gonna freeze your butts off out here."

"Believe it or not, it feels a little warm to me. Must be my Yankee blood."

"You're a freak, Chris"

"Yeah, yeah, you's guys have fun."

"Ya'll too."

"I can't remember the last time it snowed this hard around here." Tilmon said. "People act like they never seen snow before."

He scooped a big handful of snow from the top of my pick up and formed a tight packed snowball.

"You want to play war?" He asked.

"No way. Go play with *them*." I motioned to the obnoxious kids up the road. It looked like they were all making snow angels.

"I'm down," a voice behind me said. Eric had made it outside after all. He pulled a pack of *Newport's* out of his coat and lit one up. His wife hated his smoking, and he'd done pretty good at the quitting thing over the past few years, but put a few cocktails in him and soon enough, he would be outside sneaking a few drags.

"I thought you quit?" I said.

"I am...right after this one." He held the pack out to Tilmon.

"No thanks man. I don't smoke". Eric didn't bother to ask me. He knew my wife. We stayed out there shivering while Eric hot boxed his cigarette. We were about ready to walk in when the sound of screeching brakes coming from the direction of the main subdivision entrance made us hold our collective breath and wait to hear the impact. Then it came, a big boom of high velocity metal crunching metal.

"Jesus Christ!" Eric said, "That sounded like it was right there."

"It was," Tilmon pointed up my street. Everyone on the street was now looking in that direction. "Holy shit, that sounded bad. Do you want to go see?" He dropped his snowball.

"Hell no, the last thing I want to do during a black out is stand out in the middle of the road and wait for another idiot to hit us. Let's go in and call 911.

Eric crushed out the butt and we three kings headed back inside.

"What was that?" Diane asked.

"What, the crash?"

"Yes, Eric, the crash..."

"It sounded like some sort of ...crash." Diane rolled her eyes. Sometimes Eric took a few seconds longer to…process.

"Dawn, call 911 and report an accident on 28. Right at the end of the block. I don't know if anyone was hurt, but it sounded bad."

"I can't."

"Can't what?"

"Can't call anyone. My phone doesn't work. I tried calling Dad to check on the kids while you were outside but I have no service."

I quickly scanned the countertop for my phone using one of the candles Dawn had set up everywhere. I found it. No bars. No Internet either.

"What the fuck?" I shook the phone, as if that would miraculously restore service.

"Baby, watch you mouth."

Exploding suns.

Everyone started shuffling through pockets and purses for their own phones. Everyone had the same problem. Now something was rotten in Denmark. The black out could be explained by bad weather. A few phones being buggy could even be explained. AT&T sucks, nothing new. But eight cell phones with different service providers lose service less than twenty minutes after the power goes out? Now, that shit was hinky. Dawn slid her hand over mine. I could see on her face, through the wash of candle light, that things weren't adding up for her either. She was starting to get scared. Not close to losing it, that would come later, but fear was beginning to creep around us like low banking tentacles of smoke.

"Baby, listen to me. You know how folks around here act when the weather gets loopy. Everyone loses it, and the whole town grinds to a halt. You know this, right?" I tried to sound reassuring.

"But the phones?"

"It wouldn't surprise me to find out the cell towers around here aren't up to par either. Just like the power grids. Nothing works the way it's supposed to. Nobody plans for this kind of thing. I promise you, people are out there working on it right now, and we'll call your Dad first thing."

"What if his power is out too? What about the girls? What about Wyatt?"

"What about them? They're in the safest place I can think of at your Dad's. He's got his own generator doesn't he? They're probably having the time of their lives without us around. Don't freak out."

"I'm not freaking out. I hate when you say that."

"I'm sorry, poor choice of words. Just relax and drink your wine. The lights will pop back on soon and everything will be fine." I squeezed her hand and handed her the open bottle of Cabernet from the counter. She took it but set it right back down without filling her glass.

"I love you," she said

"I love you right back."

Eric gently eased his wife down the hall. I heard him try to convince her that leaving to go pick up their son from the babysitter right now was not the best idea. Eric being the rational one in a situation was another sign that we were entering the end of days. Tilmon joined Diane on the love seat, which was appropriate for them two, and started in with the syrupy sweet honeymoon talk. They did that. They were newlyweds bursting at the seams with flowery love-speak. They made the rest of us ill, and secretly jealous. They were the only ones there without children to worry about, not that they weren't trying. If those two finally hit the jackpot with all the fertility drugs running rampant, they were bound to double the population of the southern hemisphere.

The dread working it's way around the room managed to bypass the kids on the couch. Jazz continued reading *Twilight*, or whatever it was, on the only working electronic device in the room. Talia sat oblivious to the mood of the grown-ups around her and stayed captivated with her older, cooler friend. She kept asking questions just to have something to say and Jazz fielded them with ease, never once sounding annoyed. Looking at them, you would think they were at a slumber party instead of a blackout in a severe snowstorm. I wished we all had a little of that.

"So who thinks it's odd that this is happening in December, 2012?" Dave said trying to offer up a little levity.

Silence was the collective response.

The people outside were getting louder and once or twice we thought we heard screaming. The sirens started soon. The accident up the road must have been pretty bad. Without the streetlights, it had to be chaos out there, which was fine by me as long as it stayed out there. But it didn't. It came banging on my front door. At first I thought it might be the police or someone asking for witnesses to the accident but it sounded to frantic.

"Don't answer that." Dawn said. She was gripping my arm, a white knuckled grip.

"What? Why?"

"We don't know what's out there."

"Dawn, we invited a whole shit load of people here, I'm sure it's one of them."

"Our friends aren't going to try and bang down the damn door. What are they saying?"

Suddenly Talia popped up off the sofa and started down the hall toward the door. "Daddy! It sounds like they're saying Daddy. Maybe they can't find...." My wife reached out and snatched Talia back hard. Hard enough to hurt.

"Go sit on the couch, now!" she said. Talia looked from her to me, which always pissed my wife off.

"But, Dad..."

"Go. Sit." I said. She did.

"I'll be damned, they are saying Daddy." Tilmon said, "David, is that..."

"Ashley?" David said, as he recognized the voice at the door. He bolted out of the kitchen before anyone could stop him and flung the front door open.

"Ashley, baby, is that you?" The thin figure at the door collapsed into Dave's arms.

"Somebody help me!" he shouted back to the rest of us. "Bring some light! Bring me some light!"

Eric shined his flashlight on them both and we cleared a path.

Dave carried the waif figure of his oldest daughter into the living room, as the rest of us huddled around with flashlights and candles. The girl was covered in blood, dirt, and sweat. Her yellow blouse was torn and ruined. A deformity in her right arm looked like a severe radius fracture. She also seemed to be foaming at the mouth, some kind of black putrid mucus. It sprayed out all over the place when ever she repeated her mantra; "Daddy...Daddy..."

David: "Oh my God, Ashley, baby, your okay now. Daddy's here. Can you hear me? Daddy's here.

Diane: "What's wrong with her? What is that black stuff in her mouth?

Eric: It looks like motor oil.

David: Ashley! Can you hear me?

Me: David, let me see her arm. Is there anything else bleeding?

David took a second to register what I said, and let me in closer to see what I could do. I put my hand on her skin and it nearly burned me, it was so hot.

Me: Goddamn, she's burning up. David has she been sick? What the hell? Somebody go fill the tub with cold water. Shit. Her arm is broken in two places. Stop moving her arm."

Dawn: Baby, come here.

Eric: Do you have a thermometer? I'll get it.

Stefanie: She doesn't need a thermometer you jackass. She needs a doctor. We can take her with us if...

Me: No. She's not going to make it to a doctor. This fever is crazy, she feels like she's on fire. Eric, there's a first aid kit in the cabinet next to the microwave, go get it and bring it to me. Diane I need your help.

David fell strangely silent and moved away to allow Diane access.

Eric: I can't find it dude, what does it look like?

Me: Fuck! I'll get it. Somebody go fill up the goddamn tub.

Tilmon: I got it.

Dave backed up some more and I handed the crushed arm to Diane who took it with skilled nurse's hands. I ran to the kitchen and grabbed the first aid kit that was exactly where I said it was. Dawn stopped me as I turned to go back. She was gripping Talia to her side, covering her eyes and pointing to the open front door.

Me: What's wrong? Ashley is really messed up.

Dawn: Go look. (Calm.)

Me: Go look at what?

Dawn: Go look. (Less calm)

Me: Baby, we don't have time...

Dawn: Go look now! (Not at all calm.)

I looked at the door, then at my wife's face. Her porcelain complexion was fifty shades whiter even in the low light. I handed her the first aid kit and walked to the door. Standing there in the doorway, I looked around for whatever scared my wife but there was nothing there. My adrenaline was blocking out the details, but slowly I began to notice. The people that were standing out in their yards earlier were still there, but they were different. Swaying, almost oblivious to the freezing cold. Some people were lying down completely still in the snow. Huge stipple patterns of black that stood out in stark contrast to the white snow were all over the place. Like a flatbed trailer came through slinging black paint all over everything. The kids that were screaming down the street were sitting in the snow in a circle around something I couldn't see, but it was keeping them quiet, and busy. The soft orange glow of a fire painted the darkness in the direction of the wreck we heard earlier but the sirens were coming from everywhere, every corner of the universe.

Still I didn't get it.

I saw my neighbor Chris kneeling down in his yard with his back to me. A half finished snowman on his left.

Finally something normal.

"Hey Chris, what the hell is going on out here?"

He turned when I called out but his movement looked weird. Mechanical. Like someone was turning a crank to make him move. Chris was a black guy, but the black glistening smear across his mouth and chin made his skin look grey. Then I saw something in his hands. No, not just something. It was an arm. He was holding a fucking arm. A very distinct, small brown arm disconnected at the shoulder joint. Ribbons of pink and white hung from the root. The stippled black pattern in the snow sprawled out all around Chris, but suddenly it wasn't black at all. It was red. Once I made that distinction, it might as well have glowed fluorescent. It was everywhere. It was all I could see. The whole street was washed in blood. I froze and stared at my neighbor. I tried to convince myself he wasn't chewing anything. I tried to convince myself it wasn't pieces of a shredded hot pink snowsuit littering his yard.

"What. In. The. Fuck?" My head was spinning.

Chris began to crank himself up to his feet, but I was on the other side of a double locked door before he was a quarter of the way up. Dawn was still standing in the hallway where I left her. Still white as a sheet, but now she was shaking. So was I.

"What's going on?" Her voice was trembling.

"I don't know, maybe you should take Talia upstairs."

"What about the kids? What about my Dad?"

We'll figure it out, okay, I promise."

"No, This is not fucking okay!"

"Baby..."

David was frantic, "What's happening to her? Goddamn it, somebody do something!"

Diane: I'm trying! I'm Trying!

Stefanie: That black shit is getting everywhere.

Dawn: Go help her.

Me: Guys, help me move her into the tub.

Eric: Dude, something's not right.

Ashley started to shake and convulse. It took every bit of what we had to hold her. She twisted and hissed on the floor before finally falling completely still. The room was silent. With one final bubbling squirt of black saliva, that kid took her last breath. I checked her pulse. Nothing. Her eyes were completely glazed over. I started compressions.

30. Listen. Nothing.

30. Listen. Nothing.

David's sobbing was droning in the back of my skull. I couldn't think. This kid I've known since she was a baby just died on my floor and there's nothing I could do. I don't even know how she died. I stopped pumping her frail chest and leaned back. David pushed me out of the way

"Move! You're doing it wrong. Aren't you a fucking paramedic? That's my daughter, Move!" He dropped down to give his daughter mouth to mouth, but every time he tried to fill her lungs with air he came back up hacking out mouthfuls of putrid black foam. I tried to stop him. He pushed me off. He kept the compressions going for a few more rounds. He broke a few more of her ribs. It was Tilmon and Diane that finally pulled him off.

"She's gone Dave, she's gone." Diane pulled him into her arms. He fought her at first too but finally I gave in and David's world cracked in half.

The world was lost to the rest of us exactly two minutes later, when the impossible happened.

Ashley sat up.

She folded upward at the waist like a hinge and turned her head to the left, then the right, like on a crank. She opened her mouth and let out a sound carved from ice and broken glass. Diane was the first to scream, but we all followed suit. David broke free from Diane's arms and faced his dead daughter.

"Ashley?" he said, wiping tears and snot from his face. She lurched forward and dug her fingernails into his chest. Dave howled in pain. She strained her neck and snapped her jaws over and over trying to bite his face, or shoulder, whatever she could get close to. He pushed and held her back long enough for the rest of us to grab her. Her snapping teeth were barely inches from his face. She spat more fiercely now, and it mixed with the blood from his chest making everything a slippery mess.

"Jesus, Ashley, stop! Please stop! It's your Dad. I'm your Dad!" We tried to hold her back but she was so fucking strong. Tilmon had her by her fractured arm until it came off in his hands. It didn't phase this thing at all. She just swung the freed stump toward David.

"I can't hold her!" Tilmon yelled over and over.

"Somebody hit her!" I yelled back at anyone listening. We almost lost our grip entirely right before Jazz came up behind me and shoved an 8" *Rachel Ray* carving knife hilt deep into the back of her sisters head.

Ashley dropped on top of her father like a sack of bricks, dead for the second time. David just laid there in shock. We all looked silently up at this freckle faced little girl who minutes ago was curled up on the couch with a book. We stared for an eternity, all thinking the same thing. *Did that really happen?*

Dave finally broke the silence, very gently pushing the skewered girls body to the side.

"Aww baby, what did you do? What did you do? That was your sister!"

"That wasn't my sister. That was a freaking zombie."

***

Dawn was upstairs wrangling my daughter like I promised her she wouldn't have to do, and missed the entire horror show. I met her as she came down.

"Is Talia okay?"

"She wants you, but I told her Ashley was sick and you were going to try to help her."

"Nothing I can do for her now." She looked over my shoulder into the bloodbath on our living room rug.

"Did you?" she said, raising her hands to cover her mouth.

"No. It was Jazz."

"Jazz?"

"Yup."

"So Ashley...she was a..."

"Zombie? Yeah, it looks that way."

"This can't really be happening."

"My brain is telling me the same thing, but how else do we explain this?"

"Have you told them what you think?"

"I was waiting on you. Are you sure Talia is okay up there?"

"Yes, I gave her your iPad. She was over it."

"Did you check the..."

"Internet? Of course. Nothing."

David was a mess. Diane had cleaned his scratches the best she could and tried to console him, but He insisted on cradling the corpse of his dead daughter. Jazz had removed the carving knife from the back of her sisters skull, wiped it clean across her jeans, and slid it into the slack of her belt. Watching her do it unsettled everyone, but no one stopped her. Tilmon braced himself in case the corpse returned for round three, but when it didn't get up, He returned to 'stroking the majestic blown locks of his Lady Di.' Eric and Stef bypassed their glasses and were chugging bourbon straight from the bottle. I wanted to join them, but I knew it would only complicate what was coming next:

Me: Guys, We need to talk about this.

Stef: We need to get the fuck out of here.

Eric: I need a cigarette.

Stef: If you smoke a cigarette, I swear to god I'm going to...

Me: Stop. We need to stay on topic here.

Stef: And that topic is what exactly? That we have a teenage psycho in the house who killed her own sister? And nobody here seems to give a shit?

Jazz tuned in, then stared at the floor.

Me: That's not what happened.

Stef: The hell it isn't!

Eric: Stefanie chill out.

Stef: Don't tell me to chill out. I was here. We all were. We all saw what she did.

Me: Jazz did not kill her sister. She killed a zombie that was attempting to eat her father.

Stef: Are you out of your fucking mind? Are we suppose to believe..."

Dawn: Yes, you are. Now shut the fuck up, and listen to what the man has to say.

Nobody said shit. Wow. Dawn was giving me the floor. That never happened. If I had any doubts before, they were all gone now.

Hell had completely frozen over. Nobody believed what I had to say. Nobody wanted to believe it, but nobody else could offer up any explanations for what had just happened.

"Man, come on," Tilmon said, "Zombies aren't real. That's just TV shit."

"Tilmon, up until a little while ago, I would have agreed with you, but I'm pretty sure I saw people outside eating each other. I'm also pretty sure I saw a 17 year old girl die, come back, and try to eat Dave over there. We have no communication with the outside world. The phones don't work. The Internet doesn't work. We have no TV or radio offering us any other explanation to what's going on, so I'm going to assume the worse, and go with zombies.

Silence.

Tilmon chewed on that for a second. "Okay. I'm good with that."

"Me too." Diane agreed. "Now what?"

I think for once in my life I felt like the smartest guy in the room. " You know, I actually have an answer for that."

"Of course you do." Stef said, "Let's hear it great zombie hunter."

Dawn pulled her hair back in a ponytail and looked Stef dead in the eye. "Last time Stefanie. You really need to hear this. If you chose not to believe it than that's your prerogative, but lose the attitude or I'm gonna slap the shit out of you."

Stef looked to Eric for a little back up but got nothing but a shrug. Gotta love that guy. In the 17 years I've known him, he's never taken a side against me. Ever. He may not be the brightest bulb in the box, but there's a lot to be said for loyalty.

"Okay," I said, "Here's the deal. First thing we need to do is fortify the windows. The doors are oak and dead bolted so we're good there. I know everyone is worried about kids and loved ones and shit like that, but trust me, leaving this place in the middle of the chaos erupting outside is a huge mistake. We bug-in. Zombie 101.

"What does Bug-in mean?" Tilmon said.

"It means we don't bug-out. I have a stash in the walk-in attic up in Talia's room full of food and blankets. Candles, water, and all kinds of shit. The bonus room upstairs only has one way in, so we hold up and defend it.

"Guns?" Tilmon asked.

"Yeah, I got guns too. I'll get to that."

Dawn cocked her head to the side. She didn't know about my bug-in stash, but she knew me, so she wasn't too surprised.

"The zombies me and Dawn saw outside looked busy with the neighbors, but they will eventually run out of meat and start looking for more. Everything we do from this point on needs to be as quiet as possible. So that means that the guns upstairs are for last resort only. We don't want to attract undo attention. Everyone grab a knife, Jazz style, from the kitchen and grab anything you can use for a blunt instrument. Tilmon, did you fill the tub earlier?"

"Um, yeah."

"Good. Go in my room and fill the other one. In the event that the water stops, and it will, we can use it for back up drinking water or whatever."

Dawn looked confused. "I thought you said we were gonna hold up upstairs?"

"We are. The flooring in the attic is directly over the master bathroom. God forbid we're stuck here long enough to need to, we can tunnel down. It's nothing but drywall. Questions?"

Tilmon actually put his hand up. "Well, yeah. I got one. How is it that you know all this shit. I mean, don't take offense, but you seem pretty prepared for something that isn't suppose to be real?"

I stared at him for a second, and then realized Tilmon was the newest addition to this group of friends. He didn't know me like the rest of them do. I explained.

"Dude, I've been an avid zombie fan my whole adult life. *Romero, Fulci, McKinney, The Walking Dead, Max Brook's Zombie Survival Guide*, ---shit-I need to grab that. I've seen all the movies, read all the books, even the bad ones. Hell, I even gave out copies of *Word War Z* as groomsman gift's at my wedding."

Tilmon looked over at Dawn. She reluctantly shook her head.

"Believe me, if there is one thing I know about, its zombies. I can get us through this but you have to do exactly as I say. So if everyone is on the same page, we need to split up some duties and get our asses upstairs. Tilmon, fill the tub and get something over those windows. Dawn and Diane, grab anything we may need to stash upstairs, food, toilet paper, soap, batteries, shit like that. And don't forget to blow out all these candles before we head up so we don't burn our own house down. Jazz, um...grab all the long knives and go upstairs with Talia Tell her Daddy will be right up. Eric, you and me...Eric? Where's Eric?"

"He walked off, while you were talking about bugs or something." Stef said.

"Goddamn it. We don't have time for this."

"Listen," Diane said, "I'm not pretending to be an expert on zombies or anything, but don't you have to be bit by one to turn into one?

"Normally, yeah. Why?"

"Ashley wasn't bit."

"How do you know that?"

"I did a pre-trauma assessment of her before she got all, um, zombified, and other than the fractured arm, I didn't find anything but some scrapes and bruises. I would have recalled seeing a bite.

"Jesus, really? Let me see."

David allowed Tilmon and Diane to drag Ashley's body over to where we were. To be honest, David barely even moved. The poor bastard was taking it hard, and who could blame him. If I lost any of my own kids I would be...I don't want to think about it. Dawn and me looked over the body again and again. No bite. She had some light scratches across her back most likely caused by whatever chased her here, but they were barely even breaking the skin. This isn't something I was prepared for. *Could you be infected by a scratch?*

"Maybe whatever is causing it is airborne?" Tilmon said

I shook my head "No, it can't be, or else we would all be fucked already."

"Maybe only certain people get it," Diane said, "you know, like Chicken Pox."

"That's assuming a lot. We can't take those kind of chances."

"What about the spit?" Dawn said.

"The spit?" I wasn't tracking.

"Yeah, the black spit she was squirting everywhere. Maybe whatever chased her here was spewing that same shit at her."

"It's a good theory but viruses can rarely survive outside the bloodstream, so simple contact wouldn't be enough."

"For real." Stef said, "I got covered in that shit and I feel fine."

Dawn squatted down next to Ashley's body and examined her back. "What if it got in through the scratches on her back? There would be enough blood there to draw it in, especially when they were fresh."

"I guess so," I said, "It would have the same effect as a bite."

"Oh my God." She said as the realization set in.

It took a second for me to get it, one precious second that might have made all the difference. No wonder he didn't move earlier, he was either burned out with fever, or already dead. None of us noticed, and now it was too late. David pounced. He was on top of Diane before I could even finish putting my head around it. He bit down hard on Diane's shoulder with mechanical-like jaws and ripped out a mouthful of red tendons and muscle, exposing the bone. He held her tight and chewed. Diane passed out. Tilmon put every bit of his 250 pounds into the swing that connected with David's head. It knocked him across the room and would have killed him if he weren't already dead. Tilmon sank to his knees in front of his new bride where I was already doing my best to stop the bleeding.

"I got her. You need to put him down." I pointed toward David who was up and shuffling back toward us. His neck was broken from the punch Tilmon gave him and his head hung a little lopsided and bounced as he moved.

"Oh, Lady Di!" Tilmon was sobbing and wrapped his thick arms around his wife, burying his head in her blood soaked bosom.

"Tilmon! I'm not fucking around here. If I let go of this wound she'll bleed out. You gotta put that thing down!" He just cried harder. Squeezed harder. He wasn't listening to me, and dead Dave was almost on top of him. To make things worse, my good pal Eric, who stepped out to sneak a smoke during the goddamn apocalypse, was attacked by one of the fuckers outside, and damn near bust the front door down trying to get back in. I grabbed Tilmon's hand and pried it off Diane's back, replacing my own slippery palm with his, keeping pressure on the wound. I knew she was dead anyway, but I didn't want to believe I just lost three of the people I said I was going to help get through this. I didn't want to kill three more of my friends. Turns out I didn't have to. My wife did it for me. Dawn appeared at the bottom of the stairs with the 9mm I had stashed in the attic, and put the first round through David's left eye. His already wobbling head spun on its broken cervical and he dropped to the floor. Without a second thought, she spun around to the broken front door and put another round into Eric's temple. That's when I noticed most of his left leg was missing. She had no choice. The shots were louder than God in our small hallway and the noise snapped Tilmon out of his stupor. Even with my ears ringing I could hear my wife's words.

"Okay, new plan. The front door has been compromised, so we're going to lose the first floor, forget everything down here and get upstairs. What we already have up there is going to have to do. Tilmon, you need to snap the fuck out of it. Man up, and get your wife up those stairs. My husband will help. Do it now."

"Baby, she's bit."

"Help him anyway." She wanted them to have a proper goodbye. "Those gun shots just woke up the neighborhood so any minute we're going to get over run. Now move!"

Like I said, she always has a better plan.

"You shot my husband." Stef said. I almost forgot she was there.

"I did him a favor and you know it, so are you coming or not?"

"Can I have a minute with him?"

Dawn softened. "Of course you can. I'll cover you." Stef moved briskly toward the folded corpse of her man and kneeled down next to him.

Then started to search his pockets for the car keys.

I half expected Dawn to put another slug through the back of her head, but she didn't. She just sighed, and handed the gun to me. I slid it down the back of my jeans and nearly welded my ass crack shut. We got Diane upstairs right before we heard the sound of a car cranking up, glass breaking, and Stefanie screaming. The three of us looked at each other and observed a moment of silence. For Eric. He deserved better.

When we burst into the room, Talia immediately attached herself to my waist, causing us to drop Diane to the floor. My friend had the fever already and was beginning to drool black foam. I peeled Talia off me and pushed the hair back from her face.

"Stay back with Jazz, honey. Just one more minute and then I'll never leave you again, Okay?"

"Daddy, I'm..."

"Talia." I gave her the serious Dad face. "Okay?" I repeated.

"Okay." She slunk back toward Jazz who embraced her with both arms, and sat her back on the bed.

"Tilmon," I said. " She's going to turn into one of those things. We can't let that happen."

"What do you want me to do? I can't kill her. I just can't. She's my Lady Di. She's the best thing that ever happened to me."

"She's already dead Brother. If you love her that much, you need to do this for her."

"I just can't"

"Do you want me to do it for you?" A big arm shoved me back, and I fell on my ass. The gun barrel gouged into my tailbone.

"Don't you touch her!" he growled and glared at me.

"Come on Tilmon, wake up. I've known her since I was 12 years old, and love her more than most of my blood relatives, but any second now she's going to wake up and want to kill everyone in this room, and I cannot let that happen. Dawn allowed you to bring her up here to give you this last time with her, but if you don't stop her, I will. It will break my heart, but if I have to go through you, I'll do that too."

The anger left his eyes, and the blubbering wreck returned. I thought I was going to have to slap him but he pulled it together.

"Okay. I'll do it. Give me the gun."

"No gun." I said. "We can't draw more attention to ourselves." I motioned to Jazz who kneeled next to Tilmon and without a word handed him the Carving knife. He looked at me with a pleading "Do I have too?" expression. I nodded. He took the knife. We backed up to give the man space.

"I love you so much princess." he gazed lovesick into her eyes as if completely unaware of the black filth flowing from her mouth. Her arms started twitching and the mechanical movement of her jaws began. Open-open-snap! Open-open-snap!

"Tilmon, now!" I yelled. He raised the knife to her forehead. Then he let it fall to the floor.

"NO!" I tried to reach for him but it was too late.

"I don't want to live without you." He said and leaned into her, practically pushing himself into her snapping mouth. He held her tight even when she ripped his throat out. In my heart I knew it was going to play out like that. The guy was a class act, dumb as a sack of hammers, but a class act. I picked up the knife and sent them both to a place where love like that lasts forever. At least that's what

I told myself as we pushed both of their bodies down the stairs and blockaded the door.

***

My daughter was a mess. Her young brain was still trying to process the things her eyes were taking in, but it was happening at a much slower rate than the rest of us. She was a smart kid, a lot sharper than most kids her age, but less than one hour ago her biggest concern was what Chex mix to try first. Her total world experience was a trip to Six Flags, and a zombie was a Halloween mask. I was lucky she wasn't catatonic.

"Daddy, are we going to die too? Are we going to turn into monsters like Aunt Diane?"

"No Baby," I said in the best comforting tone I could muster. I pulled her across the bed into my arms. "We're not going to die, and nobody else is going to turn into a monster. You have nothing to be scared of." Dawn put her delicate hand on my shoulder.

"No,'" she said, " Don't do that. If she is going to get through this, we need to level with her. We can't afford for her to close her eyes and wait for Daddy to save the day, when she could make the difference in keeping one of us alive. Don't sugarcoat it. She's a tough kid. She can handle it.

"So we are going to die?" Talia asked and stared up at me. I couldn't speak.

Dawn answered instead. "Yes baby. Everybody dies at some point. That's just how it goes. Most people die from getting to old, but sometimes people die way too early like your Aunt Diane. But listen to me very closely, something is going on in the world right now that is causing a lot of people to die and turn into scary monsters."

"Zombies?" Talia said.

"Don't interrupt me. I told you this is important. Yes, zombies, like your Daddy's video games. Something is happening to people who get bit by one, or get that yucky black stuff on them. If either of those things happens to you, you're going to die and become one of those things too. Do you understand what I'm saying?"

"Yes." Talia wiped the tears from her face and straightened her posture to show my wife how grown up she could look.

"Good. Because it's very important to listen and do everything your Daddy and me say because that's what's going to keep you safe. Your Daddy would die for you, but we don't want him to, because we need him to keep us safe. Right?"

"Right."

"Good girl."

"What are we going to do now?" Talia asked. I found my voice and chimed in.

"We're going to camp out here in your room for a couple of days and wait for everything outside to calm down. We can play quiet games, and eat junk food. We can pretend like we're on a camping trip as long as we stay real quiet and stay close to each other. You got all your stuff in here so there should be plenty for you to do."

"Can I play on your iPad?" My first smile.

"Of course you can."

"What happens after a few days?"

"Then we head to your Papa's farm and get your sisters and baby brother." I looked to Dawn to see if that was indeed what we were going to do, and she nodded with approval.

"Do you think the zombies are at Papa's too?" Talia suddenly looked less comforted.

"I'm sure they are, baby, but I promise you, your brother and sisters are in the safest place in all of Georgia right now. Your Papa's got everything he needs there to keep us safe. We just need to get there." I looked to my wife again and got another approving nod, and a wink. Her father was a survivalist with an arsenal at his disposal. His property was easily defendable and there was a natural water source. Sending the kids there was best thing we could have done. I wish Talia was there with them. She was supposed to be. I deviated from the plan. When am I going to learn? Everything I was thinking must have been playing out on my face because Dawn took my hand.

"It's okay." She said. "We'll make it."

"Jazz," I said, " You are more than welcome to come with us." She had just finished setting the portable lanterns around the room, filling it with a soft blue glow.

"Sure. My whole family is dead. Why not?" Completely deadpan.

"Jazz..." again I lost my ability to speak.

"It's okay," she said, " Maybe once we get to your Father-in-law's house, I can have a few years to cry about it."

"Of course Kiddo."

"What about Nana?" Talia asked.

"We'll see, honey. We'll see." Dawn didn't try to correct that lie.

***

The large bonus-room Talia used for a bedroom had no windows, hence it being called a bonus-room and not a bedroom, so the only means of egress was either back down the stairs or through the walk-in attic. We could punch through the floor into the master-bath, or walk the cross beams into the space above the garage, and come out the scuttle hole. We had a way out, and a small funnel to defend if these things could figure out the stairs. They aren't sticking to traditional rules, so God help us if I'm wrong about that too.

We spent the next three days mostly huddled in a circle trying to decipher the bumps and moans coming sporadically from the rooms downstairs. It was hard to judge the time without any natural light, but jazz had one of those plastic digital kids watches, so at least we knew the time. Still no phones or power, and Talia killed the power to the tablet within 48 hours. The screams and sirens that droned in the distance on that first night started to die off and eventually faded from earshot all together. I assumed that was due to the shrinking number of living people. The dead rustled through the house below us and I felt violated every time. I did a pretty good job stocking out the attic with food and water, so even though I tried to ration us for the trip ahead, I still let Talia have whatever she wanted. Dawn barely ate at all, just enough to keep her energy up. In between all four of our bouts with anger, and emotional crying fits, we spent our time reassuring each other that we could get through this. More importantly, I taught the girls how to load, clean, and use the pump action Mossberg I had stashed with the *Ruger 9mm*. I counted about 600 rounds for the handgun and 84 low recoil shells for the 12 gauge. The last time I was up here, it looked like The National Armory. Now, it just looked pitiful. I hoped it would be enough. The plan was to leave on Christmas Day. Today. First I would do a little recon through the scuttle hole above the garage. I had to make sure my truck was clear of any obstruction before we all headed down and found out we needed another vehicle. If the path was clear, I would signal for the girls and get the fuck outta Dodge.

"Let me go with you." Dawn insisted. "I can cover you with the shotgun."

"I'll be fine," I said. " I'm just going to take a look around and be right back. Watch for me at the scuttle hole and be ready. When I set the ladder for you guys to get down, we're gonna have to haul ass, Okay?"

"I still think I should go with you. You've been telling us over and over how important it is for us to stick together, and now the first thing..." I kissed her, more to shut her up than anything, but it felt lonely and hollow. As if it were a goodbye kiss. She put her hand on her lips and became fragile as glass. I didn't let it linger. I placed another soft kiss on her forehead.

"Be ready." I said.

"We will."

I clicked a magazine into the Ruger, and racked the slide. I slid it into the back of my jeans and opened up the door to the attic. I found the hole in the drywall I cut out earlier, and crawled through it into the attic space above the garage. I waited a full minute for rustling or sounds below me, but heard nothing. I crept down the scuttle hole, careful to stay on the beams, and oh-so-quietly lifted the trap door letting in the first natural light I'd seen in days. I didn't expect to find the garage door open. I had no idea how it got that way, and I didn't care. It meant I didn't have to cut through the house to get to the truck in the driveway. Bonus. I moved the trap door upward an inch at a time, listening for anything at each increment. When I was fairly positive that the garage was free of hungry dead people, I slowly poked my head out. Shit. The garage wasn't open. My truck knocked it in. Something must have hit my truck hard enough to push it through my garage door. The truck looked undamaged from this view, but I needed to see behind it. I pulled my head back in and shined my flashlight back the hole in the drywall. That was my signal to let Dawn know I was heading down and for them to move forward. I stuffed the light back in my pocket and slowly lowered my self down into the garage. I stood frozen until I saw Dawn's face in the access hole above me. I put a finger to my lips and she nodded.

I pulled the gun out, and slowly stooped under the mangled garage door. On the other side I saw the war-zone my suburban subdivision had been turned into. Some places had been burned out and were still smoking. It's a miracle that the fires from one of the adjoining townhouses didn't take us with them. Another bonus. The snow had vanished as if it was never there, and it felt like a spring day, typical of East Georgia. Without the blanket of snow to hide the details, the death on the ground was almost too much to bear. Tattered Christmas decorations swayed in the breeze. Blood and Bodies were everywhere. Some were still moving and moaning but I only counted two on their feet. They were both at least 100 yards from me, and in the same direction, just swaying back in forth. I had plenty of time to deal with the problem at hand. A U-Haul trailer was rammed up into the tailgate of my truck. I guessed it had broken free from somebody hauling ass to get out of here that first night and it slammed my truck into the garage. Easy fix. If I could lift the tongue of the trailer myself without attracting any attention, I could guide it out of the way. The rest of the street was maneuverable. We could do this. Jesus, we were going to make it. I shoved the gun back down the familiar sheath of my ass crack, and shuffled over to the U-hauls connection hitch.

One time last summer, I needed to turn the water off to the house by way of the outside valve box. I lifted the rusty cover off the underground box and it was filled with dirt, weeds, and debris. I almost reached in to turn the valve when it occurred to me that something might be living in there, so I pulled my hand back, went inside and got a crowbar and some gloves. I stuck the crowbar into the box and moved the debris around. Within seconds, hundreds of Black Widow spiders started to crawl out, frenzied from having their home disturbed. Scared the shit out of me. Lesson learned, right?

Wrong. I didn't even feel it at first. I was too excited to find I could lift the trailer with ease. As I pulled the trailer hitch up off the street, a small dead boy, who could have been one of the twins from one street over, scurried out from under the trailer and buried his sharp little dead boy teeth into my forearm. Just enough to break the skin. I dropped the trailer back to ground and it landed on the boy's waist, nearly cutting it in half. It just lay there, all grey and rotting, moaning at me. I wanted to scream. I wanted to cry. Fuck, I wanted to laugh. Big bad fucking zombie hunter. Killed within minutes of being outside for the first time by a 7 year old kid who always swam in my pool. My mind started to overload but it all faded into one singular thought. Dawn. Save Dawn. And now, I was on a clock. I put the heel of my size 11 *Carhartt* through the head of zombie boy and crushed it like a pomegranate. I Made sure the two biters up the street still had their *Thriller* on, and swept the under carriage of the trailer for anymore fucking rats. Clear. I lifted the trailer and guided it out of the way, gently set it back down on the grass. I rolled my sleeves down to cover the wound that was just beginning to fester and headed back into the garage. I saw my wife's face in the scuttle hole. She sighed with relief. I found the ladder against the wall, and set it up. I climbed up and Dawn took my hand, helping me up.

"I thought you said we were supposed to come down to you." She whispered.

"Change of plans."

"Is the truck out of play?"

"No, the truck is good. The keys are in it, and the path is clear."

"Then what is it?" She noticed the fresh sweat on my face, and put a hand on my cheek.

"Baby, your burning up...your..." She pulled her hand back as if it caught fire.

"We need to talk."

***

So that's how I ended up like this. Tied to a bookcase with my daughter's jump rope waiting for the person I promised I would always protect to kill me. Death hurts. The fever didn't take long to burn through me, but I could feel it in every cell of my body. Like I was exploding from the inside. Soon after, there was nothing. No pain, no peace either, just...nothing. Some people say that your whole life flashes before your eyes when you die. Maybe it does if the plan is for you to stay dead. Becoming something else just made me relive the last few days of mistakes I made while trying to protect my family and friends. I let them down. I let them die. I let her die. I never expected to be able to see her again after the fever burned me out. I didn't expect to see anything, but I can. Though a milky grey I can see her. She's got Talia and Jazz behind her. They've been crying. She's got the shotgun on her back. Jesus, she's beautiful. I try to tell her that, but that's not what comes out of my mouth. I just hiss and spit at her. No matter now hard I try to form the words, it just sounds like a choking groan. I can't stop my mouth from snapping at her. I want to reach out to her but I can't. I'm still tied up. I try to relax my arms, but against my will they still struggle to reach her.

What is that smell? It's her blood. She smells so good. She's talking to me. She doesn't look frightened at all.

" I don't know if you're in there, if you can here me or not, but there are some things I didn't get to say to you before…before you passed. So I'm taking a chance there may be some of you left in there that can hear me." She wipes a tear from her eye, a single tear.

"I can hear you! I can!" I try to say, but nothing comes out.

"I know you think you let me down, let us down, but you didn't. You saved our lives. You gave us everything we needed to get through this. And I promise you, we will. Without you believing in me, being my strength, keeping me on the ground, I wouldn't have made it past that first night. None of us would have. I want you to know you're the best friend I ever had, and your kids will never forget you. Your son will know who his father is. I promise. I want you to stop worrying and let go. I got this."

I believe her. I try to tell her she saved my life the day we met, but it's pointless. All she sees is a hissing monster. I know she'll get to the farm. I know she'll find them, and keep our babies safe. I also know I've never loved her more than I do at this moment. I try to scream it at her, so she can hear it just one more time. So she knows I'm in here. I try again painfully to form the words.

I just snap my teeth, and strain for her neck.

She moves toward me a little closer, and stares into my dead eyes.

"I love you right back."

I can't feel the gun she pressed up against my forehead, but that's okay. It's all going to be okay.

The End

60

28 DAYS OF MUTILATED ZOMBIE WHORES LATER

By Ryan Sayles

ACT I –

THE SQUIRTER PROBLEM AND ANGELOU'S

ARRANGEMENT

FOR REGULAR ACCESS TO DEAD-MEAT TAIL

Hacksaw, check. Ball gag, check.

Nelson squats down at the rim of the pit and watches as beneath him five of them—three dudes and two chicks—wander aimlessly and moan. Mostly putrefied chunks of Dennis lead them like a trail of breadcrumbs into the trap. Nelson was careful to divvy up the Dennis-chum; he needs it to last as long as it can. Gotta keep up supply.

The pit was located just inside the woodland's tree line, maybe one hundred feet off the county highway. Nelson's farmstead was less than a half-mile south on that two-lane blacktop; the city was two miles north. And Dennis, a former associate of Nelson's, he now litters the road in small red sprinkles. Leading north.

The pit was eight feet deep and ten feet wide; a miracle of backbreaking labor for him to dig in the first place. *This better turn a hefty fucking profit from day one* is all he could mutter back then, spending two weeks straight with nothing more than a shovel, a wheel barrow, a lean-to camp and just a touch of coke to boost him through the worst of it. Nelson used a lot of coke back when he had it. He bled his stash dry, knowing the withdrawal to come. But that was so long ago now.

He checks the semi-auto's chamber. One in the pipe.

"Oh, good." He says around his hand-rolled smoke. Down into the pit, he tosses a small pebble. Hits the most formidable male in the head. That male looks up with those hollow eyes, his jaw half-detached from whatever fight he must have lost to get bitten to begin with, and reaches. Reaches with a pale hand that is missing three nails but still has the tarnished gold wedding ring that tied him to some broad who probably was the one that bit out his throat. Turned him.

Pointing to the neck wound on the male, Nelson says, "Bitches, right? They ruin everything." Ash from his smoke flutters down and he breaks the morning silence with a deafening *crack* of the .40 caliber. The male snaps back, his forehead and scalp flapping up as the round peels his top like a sardine can.

The others notice. Nelson just huffs out, shoots the other two men. The second one, younger than the other two by ten years easy, takes three rounds to stop jumping at the rim. He falls back, one arm chewed off at the elbow from long ago.

All the walking dead had war wounds, it seemed. Nelson figured if some hellish freak that didn't feel pain, didn't feel empathy, didn't feel remorse, just a hunger that could never be quenched, was trying to eat him like a lion on a baby gazelle, well, Nelson figured he'd fight back also.

Maybe fight so hard and fierce and wild and insane that before he lost—because they always lost—he'd be missing a limb or two like all the others.

The chicks, Nelson lets them get near the rim. He's never known a chick to squirt her black, goopy foam like a stream. They just foam like rabid dogs and shake their heads, globs of infected saliva flopping off in a wild spray side-to-side. But, one can never be too sure.

The first chick, probably hot and nubile back when she had a pulse, she reaches like she's serious to get him. Hourglass figure, long hair that must have been blonde before a year's worth of grime, blood and filth caked it into white-girl dreadlocks. Tattoos across her chest, down her arms like an artist spilled ink at her shoulders.

Nitrile gloves on. Nelson carefully inspects her arms for wet droplets of foam. Nothing he can see.

Like a mongoose avoiding a cobra bite, Nelson is quick. Slaps on a handcuff, heaves with everything he has. Her arm pops out of joint—*good, less to attack with*—and she comes up. He flips her, snaps the other on. Practice, practice.

The walking dead are slow. Romero got that bit right.

On her back, the chick snarls. Nelson slams the ball gag home, plug up that hole. Nothing but broken, red-stained teeth and oozing death anyway.

"Sweetheart, this is how it is." Nelson says, getting the hacksaw. "I've been at this for going on two years now. For your kind's comfort I've tried a variety of things. Hacksaw is the best, though it does require some elbow grease on my part. You just sit still."

One foot on her chest, he squats, lines up the saw on her shoulder. Starts in. "See, while I still had power I used a reciprocating saw. The problem with that though, is I used a home improvement model, not those types that construction crews used to score concrete. I want some zombie left, see? The home improvement model needed a battery, batteries need power, blah blah blah. No more reciprocating nothing. Blame that on the grid when it shit the bed."

The arm comes off. He discards it near a small fire he started earlier. Routine by now.

"Then I moved on to a chain saw, but those either need power from a cord—go figure, huh?—or fuel." He tries hard to make eye contact with her, says with sincerity: "Sorry, but I'm just not wasting fuel on you guys. Plus, it was so fucking messy when one got loose."

He stood, both her arms off in a pile. "Course, that might have been because I was working with a 24 inch, 80.7 cc chain saw. That fucker was built for heavy tree removal. But anyways."

The first chick lay there, armless. Gagged. She tried to stand, but they were so unwieldy after they turned. As a precaution he put on the choke collar and staked the lead to the ground. He eyeballed the severed limbs. "Sorry to waste your tats, sweetheart. But, I suppose you could really blame that on the zombie apocalypse."

Went and got the second chick. Burned all four arms. Towed the males out of the pit, freshened the Dennis-chum. Walked the newest girls back to the farm.

***

"The place was my grandparents'," Nelson says, closing the corral's gate. "They both died while I was still in prison, so, you know, I didn't get to say goodbye or nothin'."

Twenty acres, cleared and flat. The barn, the storm cellar and the house all inside a half-acre in the northeastern corner. Nelson farmed what he could, but without a steady fuel source or burden animals to do the heavy lifting, most of his property had gone to weed. His grandparents had a square thicket of trees as a natural privacy fence, which nelson enjoys. The brown patches to the south he has tried to cultivate foods that will store through the winter; potatoes, apples, onions, garlic and the like. But the bottom line is he needs more.

Thus, the harem.

Both new chicks stood there, staring. Trying to moan around their gags. Chewing on the rubber. They wouldn't get far. "Keep gnawing all you want, sweetie. By the time the rubber gives you'll have decomposed to the point where you get the 'ol railroad spike to the eye."

He pumps the pressure primer on the waterspout, hoses down the chicks. A little bit of soap, more water and they were as clean as they were going to be until the next heavy rain.

Nelson turns away, looks to the front porch. New bartering materials. Whistles. His two pit bulls come rushing over. Scrawny. There used to be three. One made way for the other two to eat.

Nelson pets them both; let them lick the remnants of Dennis-chum off his fingers. It was a small thing, but it matters the world to these pits. They eagerly take the red right off, then mooch for more.

He held each dog under the chin, said, "Angelou came by, I see. Did he beg you two off with a treat?"

The pit bulls were his frontline protection. Next would come the hot lead. Nelson walks to the porch, eyeballs Angelou's barter offering. A ten-pound bag of corn seed. A battered box of .40 caliber ammo. Two granola bars dated three years prior.

Nelson huffs. "Angelou is getting stingy." But he still gathers up the items, goes inside. Starts the fire, puts the evergreen limbs on. They smoke the best, and Angelou can see the gray trail rise above the tree line from where he is supposed to wait. Off in the distance.

Nelson hangs a small helping of venison and beans over the fire. Smokes a cigarette. Eats in front of his dogs while they twitch with hunger pains. The thin, straight whipping scars across both their flanks had taught them not to whine and beg at the table. They just watch, hope for a morsel to fall.

None did, and the silence remained heavy until a staccato knock came to the door. Angelou, here to get his end of the deal.

***

"I want a go with this punk rock one," Angelou says, practically salivating while he stares at the new chick. "You know how I love tattoos."

Back at the corral, a thick white metal fence making a loop at the south end of the barn. Good enough for a horse. Nelson eyeballs the girl. She'll be the freshest in the stable for probably a while. Fall is here; the leaves have already begun to turn, the wind has been from the north for the past two days. He's seen the squirrels fattening up. Less insects at night. His apple trees and pumpkins are coming due.

All that amounts to is he'll be making less frequent checks of the pit. Maybe once a week. The most he can hope for is another catch or two, since, among other things, he's running out for the Dennis-chum. He'd continue to peek in there. He might luck out and find another deer had fallen inside. It happened on occasion. Broken legs. Easiest hunting there is.

"How about it?" Angelou, slimy and bulbous even though there has been a shorter and shorter supply of prepackaged food in the world. But Angelou—if that's even his birth name, Lord knows Nelson isn't his—he's the type of dude to horde boxes of Twinkies and soda pop while trading anything of nutritional value for zombie pussy.

Not for the first time, Nelson wishes he didn't need to kill Dennis. Now there was a scavenger. Whatever happened to Boyle was anybody's guess. Most likely he was caught by the undead and devoured or turned. Been gone for a year now. The tweaker who went by the handle "Glorious" probably shot a bump too big to take all at once and died of an overdose. That kid was always jittery and looking over his shoulder, but he would rail out the old women like he was saving lives by doing it.

"No." Nelson says. Angelou's pinched pig's face, scraggly beard and all, dropped.

"Nelson? Serious? But I brought you some bullets-"

"Repacked bullets. Three out of that box might fire. The rest are a waste."

"You know I don't know how to tell if a bullet is factory or if it's-," He droned on, pleading. Nelson knew Angelou had no idea what he was grabbing. In fact, the bullets *were* factory. But lying to Angelou, shitting on the quality of his trade, it puts cards in Nelson's deck.

Nelson puts a finger to Angelou's chest. "The corn seed is wet on the bottom-" true "and the granola bars are past their expiration-" also true, "and if I didn't know better, you're putting on weight."

"So?"

"So you're holding out. You bring me shit supplies and then ask for my best girl?"

Angelou looks like a broken little boy, his excitement splattered like a bug across Nelson's tremendous windshield. His eyes flicker here and there. Rats conspiring.

Nelson puts one hand on his K Bar, feels the weight. "I see you examining your options, Angelou." Flash. Too fast. The knife out. Licking Angelou's nose as it gives up a tiny rose-red blood drop. "Let me remind you of what happens when a scavenger tries to cull from my herd."

Angelou casts his gaze down, adrenaline-tinged bile rising in his throat. "No- I-I never…"

"Dennis had the same look the last time he came. Brought me three MRE's that he had already opened and taken what he wanted. Got shitty with me. I caught him stealing from this very stable that night. Culling from *my* herd. *My motherfucking herd, Angelou.*"

"I ain't gonna steal no squirter from you-"

"*Try it. You'll be the next chum, I swear it.*"

Angelou's bowels quivered. He liked Dennis. Thought he was funny guy. Now the best Angelou could hope for is to fuck a zombie broad lured in by Dennis's rotting flesh.

"I won't try. I promise. I *swear* it. I won't. Never even crossed my mind Nelson I swear-"

The K Bar disappears in a flash; like Angelou just woke from a nightmare. *Poof!* Gone. Nelson steps back, smiles. "Of course you won't. Now, the punk rocker can be yours when you show up with something better. Something new and exciting. Something that will get me through the winter. For now, you get mom-jeans over there."

Angelou groans, but he came all this way. He enters the stable, finds Mom-jeans, drags her out to the barn. In there was the privacy room, complete with a bed, linens, lubricants and sex toys. Also, a shotgun mounted over the door with two shells inside. Just in case things went poorly, the directive from Nelson was simple and written where every john could see it:

Use the first shell on the zombie's face, point blank.

Use the second on yourself, because no doubt you're infected.

***

As far as Nelson could tell, none of his scavengers, while in the throes of torture or ecstasy or both ever knew he observed them on a hidden camera inside the room.

At first it poked at his stomach—though he was sure it never *turned* his stomach—but after a while he grew accustomed to it. After he awoke from a voyeuristic dream one night he knew he had taken a taste for it. For watching.

Also, even though the shotgun was there, he knew that none of his deviant clientele would ever actually *use* the weapon on themselves. So he was always ready to plug a john if it came to it.

***

Angelou finished, told Nelson he would return with something "better, new and exciting" and vanished back towards the city.

Nelson stands there, taking inventory of his stable. Mom-jeans now has a limp, but after what Angelou was doing with the pool cue stick he can understand. But there are three out of the twelve he has which have deteriorated beyond good use.

He takes his time and one-by-one examines each squirter. Nude, they moan and maybe in a zombie-way protest as he explores their skin, their folds, peaks and valleys for signs of extreme putrefaction.

The sun rotates through the air enough to where Nelson marks the three that need to be spiked and leaves the stable. Puts off the work until tomorrow. He goes inside and checks on his grow operation. On the sunny side of the barn he cultivates marijuana plants. In the house's basement he dries the weed. It's not cocaine, but the ruination of human society brings with it certain burdens.

71

Tonight he locks himself on the second floor as he gives the pits a rare treat of venison flanks. He gets high and watches as the sun creeps down on the other side of the dead world, wandering where it all went when two Christmases ago something from the bowels of hell unwrapped its present and saw that it had received dominion over the Earth.

***

And the Squirter purge.

Nelson gets up bright and early, finds the ones he's marked for destruction. One by one, he leads them out to a small fire pit lined with wood. Can of gas at the ready. Kicks away the ash of her predecessors, leg sweep to put her on her back. Foot to her chest, railroad spike lined up on the eyeball. Tap tap tap it in until he feels the back of the skull. Drives it through into the wood, knows that feeling.

Knows he's done it. So many before this one, so many planned after her.

On that final squirter, as the spike punches into the wood, giving Nelson that familiar *thwump* and the squirter's body convulses into limpness, something in the bushes snaps a twig.

Nelson's head shoots up; the bushes might be ten feet away. Spike forgotten, his hand swings to his sawed-off slung around his chest. He darts to the right for some cover as the bushes separate, Red Sea-style. A stag comes out; its rack easily eight points. Nelson instinctively eases. His fears of some psychopathic man-rapist allayed as the deer trots around.

Nelson's stomach growls at the thought of fresh venison, but the stag itself is in poor health. Patches of fur are missing. Its ribs exposed through shrink-wrapped skin. It ignores him, walks with an awkward gait. It moves in a herky-jerky fashion, trotting and then twitching into a near-stumble, a bound here and there into a slow meander.

Nor does Nelson hear it chuff. Sniff. Snort.

Nelson checks for a breeze and finds a slight one at his back. Nothing impressive but enough to bring his scent to the beast downwind. Downwind by maybe ten feet. Nelson raises the sawed-off and snaps a finger into the air. The stag looks up at the sound.

The animal has kept its right side to him the entire time, and as it looks at him full on, he can see how its left side is slightly rotted out. Caved in. One eye stares with a bleary, milky cataract as maggots swirl in the socket.

Nelson pulls his trigger. The deer's skin flaps back in a rush of tears and splattering gore. Stays on its feet. Bolts.

Moving fast for the undead. Not a good sign.

Nelson feeds another round, gives chase. He holds the sawed-off low, aims for the stag's asshole. Lets the buckshot fly, gets a few in its hind legs. The hips survive the shot, and the thing bounds off.

Barks echo from up near the porch. The pits come racing. Nelson shouts a fierce command, the dogs slide in the dirt as they slow up. Nelson has seen an animal here and there become infected, and if this deer is the one—the Typhoid Mary of Zombie-ism that can transmit the infection from species to species—Nelson doesn't like his odds of fighting off two reanimated pit bulls and remaining unscathed.

The stag banks, zigzags, jumps the stable fence, and knocks over three squirters. One female gets gored by the eight-point rack and tossed around like a ragdoll. The deer bucks, the squirter is eviscerated. She flies off, a sick line of trailing intestine zipping through the air like a roll of confetti paper at a parade.

The stag changes course, gashes two other squirters. Nelson takes aim, lets one go. The deer falls over. Mom-jeans takes most the load. Her limp is worsened considerably as her pelvic bowl and all its associated guts are blown out of her ass. She crumples forward, her upper torso swallowed by the gaping hole in her lower torso.

"FUCK ME!" Nelson roars. The pits know that voice timbre. They scramble back to the house, fearing their master's wrath.

Nelson charges to the stable, eyeing the slew of blood and guts on the ground. The other squirters amble about, stepping in it all, trailing the mess about the pen. The deer surges, gets up. Nelson draws down and the thing vaults out of the stable.

Nelson jumps the fence, follows around the barn.

The stag bounds again and lands wrong. Front leg snaps backwards, the crack of bone shatters the air like a branch falling from a tree. Nelson aims but the deer dances. Makes like a tripod at a gallop. They go around the barn, Nelson knowing he only has two shells left in the tube. The deer runs through the open barn door.

Nelson charges inside, sees shelf after shelf of fetish implement his scavengers can choose from when enjoying the fruits of his stable. He sees the crossbow. Grabs it and the roll of parachute cord Dennis used to pretend-strangle the whores.

The deer plows through a bale of hay, runs outside. Mid-stride, Nelson ties a quick knot of cord onto the bolt loaded in the crossbow.

Drops to a knee, puts the sights on the stag. Shoots for its face, happy to land the arrow through its ribcage. He lets go of the cord spool, the deer runs into the woods. The spool feeds out nearly five hundred feet before it reaches its end.

Nelson reloads, gets a one-gallon canister of gasoline, follows the parachute cord like it was the Yellow Brick Road. Like the zombies follow the trail of Dennis-chum into the pit.

Luring them into the worst situation of their un-lives.

***

Nelson's greatest fear was that the Typhoid Mary Zombie would be a mosquito or fly, just something tiny and innocent that spreads the infection to him.

Sitting at his table, the final few issues of *Ramming Barely Legal Asians* spread out along the surface, maybe freshly shaven, and then some random mosquito lands on his neck while he holds his breath and enjoys the moment. The mosquito, missing two legs since they rotted off, various spots along its compound eyes blackened with decay. Sucks his blood. Excretes the infection in there, takes off to the next mindless landing spot. Just that word *excrete* crawls up and down his spine, makes him ill.

And all Nelson knows is that his autoerotic orgasm gets dampened considerably by the fact that he starts to actively die right there, pant-less in his dining room chair. A virus sweeping through him that murders each cell only to reanimate them as something worse.

The best he can hope for is to be shot by another survivor before they fully realize he is nude from the waist down, giving them time to invent horribly embarrassing situations about his death like he does for the zombies he encounters.

How the disease that animated dead human flesh makes the jump to another species eludes him, but he knows that once in a blue moon it does so successfully. Nelson has seen dogs run around the feet of zombies and be ignored. Once, in the early aftermath of the apocalypse, he watched as an elderly zombie woman sat on a park bench as a live squirrel ate a walnut on her head.

But it happened. A fluke mutation? An occurrence every million exposures? Ten million? If every living thing on Earth became undead, there would be nowhere left to hide. In his worst fears, his deepest, darkest terrors, Nelson explored the possibility of being snatched off a woodland trail by a zombie tree. Plants live, don't they?

Just some oak branch snaking down, curled and limp bark rotting and falling like fish scales, wrapping him with suffocating brown, crisp leaves as feeder branches slither up his nostrils and down his throat. Acorns tips pricking his skin and lavishing in his hot, red blood. Feverish and moist, licking at him like he were the center of some fluid orgy.

Ridiculous if one had never seen a zombie deer goring armless, ballgagged zombie women in a converted horse stable that now houses a harem of undead sex slaves.

So Nelson follows the parachute cord as it slinks along the ground, teasing a path towards the stag which, in Nelson's estimation, carries the Typhoid Mary Zombie mutation. Considering that, Nelson decides it is better safe than sorry and resolves to kill and torch the entire stable. They've all mucked through the mess this thing caused.

The parachute cord stops trailing forward, and Nelson moves faster. He sees the cord tangled in some scraggily underbrush, continuing on through the fallen leaves and denuded plants towards a small clearing. Nelson can hear the quite susurration of the creek which runs through here growing louder. Zombie deer don't drink actual water, do they? He flash boils everything he drinks, but still. What if that wasn't enough? After two years, the thought of flash-boiling *not* killing the infection had never occurred to him. Why would it? Zombies don't drink water. They can't. Right?

Nelson breaks a sweat as his stomach rolls, leading the way with the sawed-off. He tries to control his panic. He's had to become his own reassurance, and many times he fails himself. Through a copse of trees and there it is. A lifeless stag, one leg bent to hell and its flanks chewed up by buckshot, just standing still and not drinking from the creek.

"Thank God. Or…somebody." Nelson whispers.

It cranes its head towards Nelson just as the sawed-off lines up on its head. *Boom.* Birds light off. Somewhere a squirrel shits its pants and scales a tree towards its nest. The zombie stag becomes a head shorter as a spray of coagulated innards explodes out of the back of its skull. Drops to its belly. Face obliterated. Rolls over. Nothing left.

Dead again. Dead more. Dead beyond the limits of the previous concept of death.

Nelson clears the scattered brush from the area, mounds dirt around the corpse. Douses with gasoline, lights it up. No chance for the Typhoid Mary Zombie goo to be eaten by some other animal. Spread the disease further.

When the fire consumes the stag enough to where he relaxes, Nelson lets it burn down and then mounds dirt on top of it.

Starts to leave when he sees the bold blue canvas of a tent through some nearby trees.

***

Nelson spins like a madman, checking every twist of branch and fluff of fallen leaf-pile searching for whoever owns that tarp.

"Idiot!" he shouts at himself, the eccentricities of years of solitary living showing through. One habit Nelson has subconsciously developed is talking out loud to himself. There are simply no other regular human voices for his ears to hear, save the feral, brainless moans of the undead.

"Fucking IDIOT!"

Whoever was camping under that tent would have had ample time to attack Nelson by now. The brash rumble of the chase, the sawed-off's explosion, the amount of time needed to build the pyre for the stag. The burn time itself.

Nelson might have been outflanked a solid hour ago. Observed. Plotted against. As he absent-mindedly urinated on the sizzling ashes of the deer, Nelson's head may have rested in the crosshairs of a high-powered rifle. Or a bow and arrow. There might have been a silent man coming up behind him with a knife outstretched.

"I'll fucking kill you! Show yourself!" But no one does. The woodland pasture teases him with its nothingness.

Nelson boils over with fury for being so stupid. Spits up smoking bile with indignation that this blue-tent coward hasn't come forward. Nelson charges. Jumps the creek with a rustling and a splash, barely feels the ice cold water dart up to his knees as his eyes zero in on the tent. One blast shreds it, sends it flapping to the ground.

If he weren't out of shells he'd waste good buckshot with another blast. Nelson surges to it, possessed by the ire and humiliation of his non-observance. The *could have been's* of the

77

situation. He throws the canvas back. No blood. No people. Cold ashes. Trash.

All alone.

***

A small jar of oily-feeling white stuff, smells like coconut oil solids, baking powder and maybe cinnamon. Patchouli for sure.

There are scratches through the goop about a finger-wide, like he used to see on a balm or cosmetic. Homemade. *Hippie deodorant.* Nelson sets aside the jar, tosses the rest of the junk. Not much else. Some reused paper, several squares of cloth laundered until they've frayed at the edge. *Hippie toilet paper.* Even post-apocalypse these dipshits think they need to recycle. A little bit of weed. *Hippie enlightenment.*

Nelson picks through the stems and seeds, finds little else. "I've throw out better grass."

One hefty mountain climbing backpack, situated on an aluminum frame. A photograph of a man and woman, white, early twenties. Shaggy hair on both. Nelson can practically smell them from the photo. The male looks like he abuses estrogen pills and the female looks like she has a facial piercing fetish. She's be pretty if she weren't such a freak.

The photo has them posing ferociously in their name brand winter coats at some festival or sit-in. Maybe a Million Faggot March. Night lit by street lamps and camping lanterns, illuminating their fogging breath. People in the background on iPads and iPhones, tweeting about how much they hate The Man. Huge buildings behind them. Tent city. Occupying some park, somewhere, sometime.

Nelson imagines them perching in a tree somewhere to keep it from being cut down. Dropping baggies of poop on people who come too near. Or accosting at folks driving SUV's. Or building mud huts to live in, eating bugs and twigs and thinking they're making a difference.

Well, they got their world back. The planet won't know bumper-to-bumper traffic for centuries, or billowing smoke from factories or animals being raised just to be turned into food en mass.

Nelson looks around for signs of existence, or evac. There are things to return for. But the camp seems hastily departed. Something spooked them. Maybe they ran when the shotgun blast sounded. Maybe they ran when the infected stag showed up. It might there is something else Nelson doesn't even know about.

He sees blood. A blob of it on the ground, smashed leaves and scuffled dirt. Nelson uses a twig to touch the mess. Tacky, but old.

No drag marks. A sprinkling of red here and there. No discarded bandages. Whoever bled started and stopped here. No trail of it leading off. Maybe they fought over something foolish—like the weed—and when it was done, they decided to go for a walk. Perch in a tree. Poop in a bag.

The stream leads north to the county road in less than a mile. The county road leads back into the city. Maybe they went back. Who cares. Gone now. Dead deer.

Nelson takes the hippie deodorant, the picture, the pack—it's still in good shape—and he treks home.

***

Arriving back at the farm, Angelou is waiting with such a large grin Nelson is instantly concerned.

Also, Angelou's belt is already undone.

"This is not how it's done, Angelou." Nelson asks, one hand touching his sawed-off. "What are you doing here, breaking my rules?"

Angelou can barely contain his hubbub, points to the front porch, asks, "Is that new and exciting enough for ya?"

Nelson sees the trade item. Tied up. White female, early twenties. Shaggy hair. He can practically smell her from here. Facial piercing fetish. Would be good looking if she weren't such a freak.

"Is she alive?" Nelson asks, not sure if he wants to hear yes or no.

"Yeah, buddy."

Nelson half-grins. "Well, I *did* ask for something to get me through the winter."

ACT II –

PREGNANT ECO-TERRORISTS AND THE INALIENABLE

RIGHTS OF ROTTING, LONG-DEAD PEOPLE

Nelson leaves the gag in place.

Reaches through her shaggy, dreadlock-ing hair, tugs at the rear of the gag, squeezing it between her molars. Face an inch away, he says, "Just so you know who's boss."

Leads her inside. Gets her to where he wants her. Thumps her in back of her knee, breaks her stance. Collapses. On the floor, she sits up, adopts a Zen pose even though her eyes burn with a scathing hatred. Nelson sees this. Smiles. Examines her head for a wound which would bleed like what he saw at the camp. None.

Eats in front her. Tosses a few spoonfuls at her. They splatter uselessly across her chest, lap. The pits come along, lick it off.

Nelson washes his bowl. Comes back. Sits down at the table and makes himself comfortable. Sticks his finger in her mouth and hooks the gag. Yanks down and forward. Her chin bounces off her chest, she rocks forward enough to grind her knees along the hardwood floor. She coughs, mouth free.

"Your hand tastes like dick, you fucking pervert," she says with her acid-drenched, parched voice. Nelson says nothing, then claps her upside the head so loud the dogs run away. Unconscious, she slumps over.

Nelson gets up, goes into the kitchen. Makes himself something to drink. Warm up. After two cups of coffee she regains consciousness. He stares at her.

"Feel like starting over?"

She seethes, tears welling in her eyes. "No."

"Well, let me rephrase that. Now that you understand how sensitive I am to slights, I assume unless you want to become a human toilet you will respect my delicate nature."

She says nothing. Can't fight her tears.

"Cry if you want. Hopefully those tears will wash off the stench of BO and essential oils."

Still nothing. She fights her tears, looks brazen enough for her situation. Then, "Why are you so cruel?"

Nelson smirks. "You sound like my ex-wife."

She spits on his boots. "Blessings to her for jumping on that grenade in the first place. I can tell she realized you were an establishment pig who gets off on subjugating women and-"

"She loved it."

"No woman loves it. They may say-"

Nelson grabs her jaw and holds her mouth shut with a squeeze. "Please stop referring to my wife in the present tense." He stares hard. She looks away. "She and my *dear, sweet* mother had two things in common. One, they were cunts, and two, they both couldn't help but love men who needed to hurt them. When you love someone for something they do, you love *it*. And Bridget, she loved it."

He lets go. Waits for the challenge. None comes. "And *soon*, you will love it as well."

She snorts. "I *love* nothing under the command of human intentions."

"Fucking hippie talk. Would it kill you hopheads to make sense every once in a while?" He sits. Stares. Studies.   "I found your tent in the woods."

"I don't have a tent."

"Right, right. The tent belongs to the world and you're just being a good steward for it. The look on your face betrays your lie." Like he's teaching a foolish student. He stands, gets the pack. Brings it to the table, presenting evidence at trial. Pulls out the hippie deodorant.

"Yours?"

She shakes her head. He leans in, smells her like some mangy dog smelling an unattended baby in a fairy tale. Savor the essence. Let it make his mouth water.

"Not your pack either, eh?"

She shakes her head again. Looks out the window at how the sun is sinking so fast.

Nelson grabs the crown of her skull the way basketball players could hold a ball in one hand with their long fingers. Turns her head to him. Hold up the photograph, folded in half. The man in the picture faces her, smiling. "Yours?"

She says nothing. He looks at her half of the photo facing him. He leans back, unfold it. Scrawled on the back are two words. Names. "Which are you, Henna or Revolution?"

She fixates on his feet. How her defiant goober slovenly runs down the side. Just wanting to stare at something. Absently she says, "Henna."

"This dude is named *Revolution*?"

"Yes."

"Were your parents hippies as well, or did you two attend college in Berkeley and take up some bullshit cause? Trust fund babies? Need some meaning in your life somewhere? Are your birth names Isabella and Mason?" A dry laugh.

"I don't need a trust fund or a university education to know Mother Earth is hurting. Dying."

He rolls his eyes. "Something tells me that whore will be just fine."

"Look around you. She is in agony."

"Well, Mother Earth got the last laugh."

"That's what I thought…"

He stares nakedly, waiting to hear her comment. She just blinks and tries to get lost in the sunset. "Until what?"

Gazing at the barn, "Until I saw your flock of abused women outside."

***

"I'm a pimp," Nelson says. "What else good are they?"

"They're still human."

A laugh. Belly-rolling laugh. "Their pussies feel human, but that's where the similarities end."

"You've been given a chance to redo your life here, to be a better man. Look at all of those who died horribly when it struck and you- you make it and you are still a rotten, soulless man that abused women-"

Nelson squats down in Henna's face. Something acrid on his breath scared her. Like impending death it washes across her, filling her nostrils and burning her eyes. "Somebody made the dead come alive, honey. If the government didn't do it and God didn't do it then Mother Fucking Earth did it. And she doesn't love you. She wants you dead. She sent your mammy and pappy from their graves to fucking eat you. Sorry."

Henna holds her head up, sets her jaw. "Be proud of your career as a zombie pimp."

Nelson fumes. Henna readies herself for her death. Moments pass like she was spinning on a circus wheel and Nelson was throwing the daggers. At some point one would land, and when it did it would skewer her face.

But the daggers don't arrive.

Instead, Nelson swallows his fury. "We all must do things to survive. That leads me to two things. First, you. You will do what you need to survive here. As my fancy dictates, so will you respond. If that is disagreeable, just let me know. I will go to the stable, scrape up some of those squirters's foam and let you slurp it up. After you turn, I will remove your arms and add you to my collection."

"And what if I run?" She sits up straighter, smug. "I am at home with nature. Do not underestimate what the Mother will do to help me. She gave us that creek, we found wild plants to eat, we-"

"Yes yes," Nelson says, lighting a smoke. "How you anthropomorphize all the sticks and dirt around is a comforting delusion." Dismissively he waves a hand. "If you run my pit bulls will eat you. In the middle of the night, while I'm bathing, checking the pit, whenever. I keep those dogs starved for a reason. Don't give them an excuse to dine on you."

He smiles. "Now, where was I? Ah. Two, the things others do to survive. I got out of the pen three weeks to the day before the apocalypse set upon us. I know how to survive in a hostile environment. I never had time to get used to society again before society devolved into this…silliness.

"I gathered to me others who knew how to survive. You've already met Angelou. He and others scavenge whatever they can find and bring it to me. In turn, I provide them with the service you see here. Little pets with nothing better to do than be a part of a fantasy. You will see them come and go. Ignore them. They will ignore you."

"Will they? How long do you think it will take for guys who fuck dead bodies to desire something alive?"

Nelson considers this for a moment. "How did Angelou capture you?"

She snickers. "Snuck up behind me while I was peeing. What a man."

"Peeing? Don't you mean you were recycling Mother Nature's water or something? Giving back what you borrowed from her for life-sustainment?"

"You're not very good at mocking."

A different tactic to hurt her, then. "It is nature's design to feed off the weak and powerless, my dear Henna." Nature as a mean-spirited thug. "Lionesses hunt the slowest of the herd. The youngest. Whatever has hot blood and got left behind. Think of the birds that return to empty nests while a snake has a full belly elsewhere. Or the toad that eats two insects while they're tied up mating."

"Whatever. You're all scoundrels and abusers."

"Of course we are. Anyways, it's really been whittled down to just Angelou now. He makes very regular visits. Set your clock to 'em."

"Don't care."

Quiet descends. Nelson has so many questions to ask the girl, but he has other things to do. This unexpected surprise has thrown him for a loop. "And what of Revolution? Did Angelou get the jump on him as well?"

"Ask Angelou."

Nelson shows his amusement. "I will. Did he get first dibs on you? Taste the honey before I arrived?"

"That bulbous pig? Please. Even if his little dick wanted to, he was so out of shape hauling me here he couldn't have acted on it." Henna struggles between telling the man to go get his foam and plotting on how she can sneak around or bribe the dogs. Her decision plays out on her face, and Nelson is satisfied.

"Good girl. Examine your options. See there are none but to obey my will." He bares his teeth in some grin, impassable as a smile. "No option but *to love it*."

Henna shakes her head, looks away.

Nelson licks his chops, asks, "Will I be meeting Revolution soon? Knight in shining armor-type thing? How chivalrous is a man who cries every time he sees a soda pop bottle in the trash rather than the recyclables?"

"Revolution is dead," is all she would say.

"Dead by Angelou's hand? Zombie bite? Smoke some bad weed? Did he commit suicide after realizing he'd never be able to watch *An Inconvenient Truth* ever again?"

She would not answer.

"Did he leave you for a chipmunk? Is that it?" Nelson lowers his voice, mocking his sympathies. "Was that his blood I found at the camp?"

Still nothing, but he thought he saw just a little, fleeting something in her eyes. Here and gone.

"How old is this photo?" He holds it up, examining it against her now. "You look like you have gained weight since."

She says nothing, and Nelson believes that is her custom. He flicks the photograph down onto the floor near her. Says, "When I get back we'll get to know each other."

He is gone.

Henna looks down to her belly, where all her weight is, whispers, "I won't let anything bad happen to you."

***

Angelou has finished with the tattooed squirter and is shoving her back in the stable as Nelson comes out.

"Where did you get the girl?"

Angelou looks nervous. "I uhhh... followed her-at a distance, mind you... from the country road into the woods. You'd be surprised how close they were to you... They had set up camp by the creek and-"

"Who is *they*?"

"She was with a dude. Some scrawny queef."

"What about him?"

"I hit him with a log. He's dead."

"Define *dead* for me, Angelou. Did you beat his face until you saw his brains?"

"No."

'Did you strangle him for a few minutes after he stopped fighting back?"

"No."

"Define *dead* then."

"He was bleeding like a stuck pig. He moaned and rolled around for a minute. I hit him like four times and he stopped moaning. Just laid still. I've hit enough dogs over the noggin in my time to know-"

"Go check, Angelou."

Uncomfortable. "What?"

"I said, *go check*." Nelson steps forward. "If I find out you kidnapped a girl from her boyfriend and he comes here looking for her I will kill him and then I will feed you to the stable. I don't want the headache."

"Even if he's alive you'll be okay. It's not like he's special forces or-"

"He might show up in the middle of the night and start a fire, Angelou. The girl said he's a firebug. Or maybe he has a hunting rifle. Did you ever consider how a scrawny queef has stayed alive for two years, keeping the girl safe as well? Yeah, he *might* be lucky, or he might be trouble. So go fucking check."

"Okay. Okay." Angelou is scared. He never considered that the guy might be trouble. He was so lanky. Covered in cheap tattoos. Hell, even the girl has that blue square with the yellow equal sign tattooed on her arm. Dirty scum. Smokes pot. Probably worships kabala or Scientology or some such nonsense. "I'll go look."

Nelson raises a stern finger. "Angelou, listen very carefully and do exactly as I say. If he is alive, kill him. If his body is still there—and the undead haven't gotten to it—cut off his head. If he's gone, find him or don't come back."

"No, Nelson. No-"

"Yes. Get it done."

Nelson knows with the threat of being cast out, Angelou will work harder. They go their separate ways, and the sun gives way to the night.

As Nelson nears his house, he hears Angelou whining, "But he's *dead*, Nelson. He's dead."

***

Revolution is not dead.

He stands just inside the tree line near the home, eyes following both men as he sizes up their capabilities.

For as many times as that fat slob hit him in the head, he did remarkably little damage. Yes, Revolution lost consciousness for a moment—who wouldn't, getting clobbered like that—and head wounds are notorious for bleeding, but the amount he lost was deceptive. That rodent of a human being wouldn't know his mother's middle name, let alone how much split blood constituted death. Headache boarding on migraine, yes. Beaten into the grave? Hardly.

Revolution always considered himself a man of few words. Words did nothing. Actions. Actions did everything. And so now, actions would win Henna's freedom. Revolution wasn't stupid; he knew he was on enemy territory. Two on one, four on one if you counted the pit bulls. Not to mention the zombies in that barn fence, or the firearms. This would need to be played right.

Best to divide and conquer. Revolution was no military-trained strategist, but he knew what worked when he was fighting for Mother Earth. Tricks, deceit, misdirection, come in low and go. Let his enemy's hubris be his demise.

The rodent is no problem. He can be easily dispatched, or used as bait. The other man, he oozes confidence and narcissism. Revolution begins to think about how he can trick. Hubris will walk its owners into such foolish snares.

As Nelson goes inside, Revolution watches Angelou stick to patches of moonlight, shuffling his bulk towards the old road. Revolution sticks to shadows, follows him.

In Revolution's hand the same log Angelou beat his head with, quietly turning in anticipation of another battering.

***

A half-mile down the road and Revolution closes the distance considerably.

"Excuse me, good sir," Revolution says. Angelou startles at the voice, never sees it as Revolution bats him across the head.

Drags him off the road a little bit, sets down his pack and withdraws what the military and police used to call an improvised Explosive Device.

Gets to work.

***

Nelson wakes in the night as light plays off his ceiling.

The heavy quilt is lulling with its heat. He adjusts his arms underneath it, snuggling in its comfort and with bleary eyes watches the watered-down tinted colors dance and flicker. Coming from outside. Nelson is mid-dream when the strange light draws him from sleep.

A gentle yellow swirls, like ripples on water. It snaps to life here on his ceiling, flirts with an orange and then blinks out. Appears over there next, pulls a red over itself like a coat. Then gone. Reds pop up and do the same. So do the oranges and then mixtures and-

Nelson is up, feet hitting the cold hardwood. With his bounding both the pits startle awake. Nelson sees his bedroom door nudged open and the mutts lying in his dirty clothes.

"Get the fuck outta here! How many times-" Distracted, he goes to kick a dog when his eyes fall upon the sight out on the lawn. He stops. Looks. Runs downstairs, gun in hand, dogs forgotten.

On the lawn there is a giant arrow of flame pointing to the road.

***

Nelson recognizes this for what it is.

A trap. Hippies think they're so clever. So *underhanded*. Rushing, interrupted sleep still sticky in the corners of his brain, Nelson ticks off what needs to be done.

Inside. Opens the door to the bathroom, finds Henna asleep where he tied her to the toilet. Her eyes flutter, "W-what?"

Nelson yanks her up to her feet. "Do you take me for an idiot? A moron? How stupid do you think I am? I know exactly what's happening here! I'm going to fucking kill him! Got me? I going to fucking *kill him!*"

90

"What are you talking about-"

"I know your shitbag boy-toy is alive! He thinks he can come here on my property- I'll gut him in front of you and eat his godda-"

"I knew it!" Henna smiles just long enough for Nelson to backhand her. Even with the thin trickle of blood down her chin, she cannot fight her smile.

Nelson leans in, almost conspiratorial. "He thinks he's setting a trap for me. Just lead me off down the road so he can scurry right in here, under my nose and steal you. You fucking stinky jackoffs have no idea what is coming. I will feed him to the squirters. You just watch me."

"You'll fail." Henna says, calm. Much too calm for how Nelson is screaming, glowing red from fury. She smiles; hearing that Revolution is alive is such relief, playing out on her face.

"Excuse me?" Smoldering, just below the level of volatile.

"Just kill me." Henna looks bored almost. "Do it now while you're still alive to do it."

The indignation is overwhelming. A thousand retorts rush through his head like a scattering of leaves in white water rapids. Everything from laughing to beating in her face come to mind, but finally, nearly against his will, he simply says, "No. Too easy."

Henna shrugs. Time to make the big man feel small. "Revolution isn't some random tree hugger, sweet cheeks. He doesn't protest outside of burger joints and complain on a blog. Revolution was on the FBI's Terrorist List before the fall of man. He burned down two ski resorts in Colorado when they cleared thousands of acres of woodland to make room for bunny hills and chairlifts. All bullshit.

"We were protesting on a road in Oregon and some dickhead in a giant SUV tried driving through us. Revolution drug the driver out of it and beat him into a coma. That consumerist, so smug while he mindlessly quaffed precious fossil fuels to drive around a house. Just one tank of gas in that senseless carriage would have powered a poor village's generator for a week. Think about it. Folks living under mosquito nets eating hand-to-mouth, hoping to survive past eighteen and that asshole was-"

"Shut up." Nelson stops to think of his next move, trying to stay calm in the midst of the blatant violation, the threat.

Henna is empowered, knowing her Revolution has begun his move. His action. "We fought against the zombies that commercial society made out of man before this infection or whatever made real zombies out of them. If you ask me, Revolution was fighting this fight his entire life. He was born for it. There is no difference between slave masters like you and the corporations which infected humans with the need for purchase power and credit and bigger, better, faster and unnatural-"

"I said *shut up*," Nelson says, lifting her to her feet by her hair. "I will not stand here and listen to some twat who used to throw red paint on women wearing fur tell me that on my own turf, according to my own rules that her fuckface little boy-toy who is so brave he attacks cars will defeat me. I *will not*."

"Fine." Henna looks away. Reserved to the fate she knows will be swinging at her face any moment.

Instead Nelson keeps hold of her by the hair. Goes outside.

***

Electrical zaps push the squirters away as he finishes the set-up.

Dawn is wiggling its deep pink fingers on the horizon. The air smells like burnt grass. Nelson closes the chicken wire entrapment and stands back, cattle prod in one hand.

"And God said *it was good*."

"You're God now?"

"Well, I'm no *mother earth*, but for the purposes here—you know, dangling you between life and death, running the show, etcetera—I am God. A vengeful one, at that."

"Okay, sure." Henna says. "What a god you must be, seeing as how Revolution came right to your front door while you dreamt like a little child."

They're in the stable. Nelson drug her to the middle of it, hogtied her to a ground stake and drove it into the middle of the pasture. Wrapped her in chicken wire and intentionally made of a mess of it. *It'll take that fuckface Revolution longer to snip through the mess and retrieve his gal-pal here, all the while fighting off the product.*

A squirter comes up to Nelson. They always want to bite, but never seem to notice they're ballgagged until it's too late. He cattle prods her, then does a leg sweep. She falls on her back. He leans over, yanks the gag free. Instantly her mouth foams up with a black, rabies-worthy goop and the look in her eyes goes from unengaged to ravenous.

Nelson backs away and leg-sweeps the next one. Henna watches as he goes down the line, finding them where they are and ungagging them. The women struggle on their backs—wasn't that always there plight, though?—and by the time the first one is able to get to her knees—oh, the irony—he is done with the last.

Out of the stable. Locks the gate. Nelson admires his work.

"Hope Revolution enjoys the obstacle course." He turns away, then turns back. "And don't worry, the chicken wire is too thick for them to bite you. Just don't swallow any errant foam which may drip on you and I think you'll make it until I return."

"What then?" She calls, dubiously. "You'll be my rescuer?"

"No," Nelson says, patting his sawed-off. "I'm going to shoot you and then let the pits in." he laughs, the harsh sincerity in his voice plain to the ear. "What did you think I'd do?"

"I have a baby in me, you know. Innocent life."

Nelson looks at his watch even though time is, for all intents and purposes now, moot. "They won't care."

The squirters thrash on the ground. Hungry. Becoming vibrant.

"Nor do I." Sawed-off shotgun in hand, Nelson strolls at a determined pace to boldly find where Revolution's burning arrow pointed to. The ruse being of course that he would actually just travel a mile or so down the road and double-back, knowing his eco-terrorist opponent will be at the stable shortly.

But not too far down the road, Nelson sees another scorned black patch of grass pointing right at Angelou, just off the road's side.

Angelou's face, beaten and more ugly than even his own mother could love, he looks up from where he is slumped in a dirt mound and says through only half his teeth, "Nelson? Can you help me?"

Nelson clenches his jaw and comes over. A moment later and Nelson regrets this.

***

An unnerving click and Nelson swallows hard, asks, "What did I just step on?"

Angelou's face twists like he just realized his bad dream is actually real. Like he just put two and two together and the sum total is shit-your-pants worthy. "Well…Nelson…you gotta understand I was- I was in and out of sleep-see…he hit me in the head…*hard* and- and-"

"*And what!?*"

"And he…buried somethin' there…I didn't think too much…"

"Did I just step on a fucking *landmine*?"

"You mean like bomb? I don't- but then again…he hit me so *hard* and- I dunno. I saw it just a bit…it was like a dinner plate…"

Nelson carefully kneels down, careful not to move his foot from where the click and sinking sensation came from. His knife out, he digs gently. Scraping around in big circles, working his way inward. In time, he finds metal.

"Pressure mine," he grumbles to himself. "IED."

"ID? What's that-" Angelou asks, leaning as close as he can.

Nelson backhands Angelou away. Angelou holds his mouth like a slapped wife and sobs just a little.

"IED. Improvised Explosive Device, dipshit." Nelson stands, starts looking around. "It's a bomb some shitbag cooked up in his garage. Doon coons would plant these things all over the Middle East and just wait for the Great White Paper Tiger to come along. Fucking slants over in Vietnam did the same shit during the war. This treehugging nincompoop piece of fucking trash hippie decks you and buries one right next to you and you're too fucking stupid to warn me before I step on the mother fucker. How stupid are you?"

"Nelson, I-"

"Shut up."

Nelson's eyes suddenly settle on a thought in his mind. They narrow; his lips quiver. Feral. He looks at the sweaty, bruised blob of a man before him, says, "Are you tied up or something?"

"Yeah."

"Let me see."

Angelou's girth flops and rolls; Nelson sees Angelou's hands are a light shade of purple as they are bound at the wrist by hemp cord—ha ha—and staked to the ground.

"Get up in a squatting position, Angelou."

The next few minutes are grotesquely comical as Angelou plays a delicate dance of shifting his blubber from one crux and vantage to the next. His feet wind up underneath his body, his rounded shoulders being pulled by the stake while his front tries to flex and sit forward.

"Turn your back to me."

Angelou rotates in that awkward side-step-side-step like a frog until his back is exposed to Nelson. Nelson takes his free foot and gets ready.

"I count to three, and you stand up as hard and fast as you can. Shove your body forward."

"Okay."

"One. Two. THREE." Nelson kicks. Angelou shoves up. The kick lands squarely between Angelou's titanic shoulder blades. With a gasping *humpfff* Angelou stands and falls forward, the tremendous yanking pulls the stake free. He falls forward and rolls away a turn or two. Comes still.

"Now get up and come over here." Nelson has his knife ready.

"What are you gonna do to me?" Angelou asks, sitting up and looking very wary of such an angry, rage-filled man.

"I'm going to cut your hands free. And then you are going to help me off of this thing."

Angelou struggles on his ass, rolls a bit, finally stands and loses his balance. Falls. Nelson openly laughs. Angelou looks genuinely hurt by the mirth. But he stands again, this time he remains on his feet.

"Come over here," Nelson says through gritting teeth, snapping his fingers and pointing at the ground before him like he's ordering a dog. His eyes burn onto Angelou as the grown man trembles like an abused dog.

Nelson can see Angelou's thoughts stream across his face like a news ticker. *Should I go over there? Will he hurt me? Can I trust him? Maybe I should just*

"GET OVER HERE YOU FAT FUCKING NO GOOD WASTE! How did you ever survive this apocalypse? You probably got fired from every greasy spoon you ever bussed dishes for because you are so incompetent you can't even follow simple directions and shuffle your fat ass over here to help get me out of this mess you put me in! GET OVER HERE!"

Angelou hesitates, knowing he will be beaten like an unruly pet if he goes over, but some strange form of loyalty keeps him from just running like his gut is telling him to do.

Nelson shrieks, "This is all your fault! Get over here!"

"Promise you won't hurt me?" Meek. Submissive. Afraid.

"Damn it, Angelou. We are not in some abusive domestic relationship. I'm not going to coddle you and tell you how beautiful you are after I manipulate you and smack you. Just come over-"

"I need you to tell me you won't hurt me. Just say that. Just *say* it."

Nelson sees it play on Angelou's face. The kid's old man must have been heavy-handed. Nelson sighs, realizes he must play-act to get the spooked mutt back to him. "All right, fine. I won't hurt you. Just come over and let me cut you free so we can both go back to the farm. Please?"

Nelson despises saying *please*. Despises.

Angelou creeps over. Gets within reaching distance. Nelson is slow, methodical. No startling moves. Like approaching an easily-spooked animal.

"Let me see your hands."

Angelou considers the leap of faith he must take to be free. Trusting such an angry man at his back. An angry man with a knife. Angelou swallows hard, reserves himself to being stabbed, and turns around. Offers his hands.

Nelson raises the knife. Fury burns in his eyes and he twitches, starts to swing downward. Catches himself as Angelou says, "I trust you won't hurt me."

Nelson's broiling desire to gore this fat fuck and roll his body weight onto the IED so he can get back before Revolution gets the girl and escapes into the never-never land all around them, it becomes tempered with the reality that Angelou is loyal, and keeps him stocked with food and supplies. Angelou does the lowly dirty work Nelson can't stand doing.

He should expect this mangy dog to tremble when its master becomes angry. There is a time for beatings and discipline, and there is a time for mercy. Mercy earns loyalty. Discipline hones it.

Nelson cuts Angelou's hands free. Angelou turns around, vigorously rubbing his wrists. "Thank you thank you thankyouthankyouthankyou-"

"Shut up. Get me a rock or something to put on this IED." Nelson says coldly. Angelou's graciousness melts some.

"Get a rock and then we'll go back to the farm. I'll reward you with whatever Squirter you want."

"Sure, Nelson, Whatever you want me to do."

"Hurry the fuck up. I'm tired of being the only one in our arrangement to do any real work."

Angelou stops, stares back at him. Could Nelson mean that?

"I said hurry the fuck up." Nelson feels good being cruel. Mercy earning loyalty or not, he convinces himself this treatment is discipline. "GET A MOVE ON!"

But Angelou was stuck on the real work comment. Dark, cold nights flash through his mind. Two years' worth, actually. Watching his family eat each other while he hid in the upstairs closet. Days inside that thing, pissing and shitting himself, scared to fall asleep because his four year-old nephew was dead-alive, trolling up and down the hallway for a few days sniffing the air like he was a wolf following a scent. The boy's legless stumps drawing gooey lines of stiffing blood along the wood floor, that eerie wet slide while he sloshed through it again and again.

Angelou's sister—the boy's mom—had turned and eaten that kid from his feet to his thighs. Then she disengaged, wandered off into the night through the shattered picture window in the living room.

How Angelou, driven by hunger and the basic need to not smell feces and ammonia, how he finally took the coats off the rack, removed the rod and beat the little kid to his next death with it. Years of dodging the living dead. Snooping through dumpsters and abandoned houses for anything he can trade for a little human contact.

Sure, he bought zombie pussy with it, but those few minutes he could talk to the other scavengers or Nelson, such a strong, resilient presence, a man who retained his humanity through this whole debacle, it made it worth it.

Real work? Nelson had never been raiding a restaurant kitchen to purchase a little human interaction when he turned around and there was a man with no eyes or nose whose hands were inches from his neck. Never fell over with that thing on top of him, smelling the rotting everything from his breath to the rancid tissue in his hollow eye sockets. Never had nightmares for weeks just hearing that breathless desire to eat him, never felt the little trickles of stagnant drool fall on his neck while he struggled against it. Never used a ballpoint pen to shove into its ear hole until his finger pushed so hard half his finger went in the hole also.

Real work? Nelson never ate something spoiled and had to take an emergency poop behind a burned-out clothing store when four of those zombie-things came around the corner. Never had to leap up to the fire escape feeling the wet slop hit his inner thighs, never had the indignity of running from certain cannibalism with shit streaked down his legs. Never pulled his excess weight to the unstable roof of the building, equally scared that he would fall through and break his back or impale himself on something and be eaten alive. No rain in sight to wash him off.

Real work? Angelou had stories. Close encounters galore. Nights soaked in his grown man tears, scared to death. Desperation to find something with which he can approach the living.

Real work? Angelou thinks not.

In the fastest move of his life, Angelou grabs the sawed-off, yanks. Nelson so startled by the move that he almost comes off the IED, pulls back. The weapon slung around his chest snaps off the harness as one man pulls forward and the other pulls back.

Nelson, stunned. Angelou, stunned as well.

"What are you going to do?" Nelson asks.

"Make sure you don't kill me." Angelou pumps out the shells, throws them one by one into the woods all over. Nelson watches silently, incredulously. Angelou uses an old key ring he still has—the things the living hang onto now that the world has ended—and uses it to push out a lynch pin in the gun. Takes it down to two pieces.

Tosses them.

"Now I feel safe," Angelou says, lets his guard down. "I'll look for a rock."

"Not a rock, Angelou. *We'll need more weight than that.*" Nelson says. He withdraws a revolver tucked in his pants at his back. Shoots a single round. Angelou's right shin explodes out the back of his leg. He screams like a rabbit in the jaws of a dog right before that final bite comes down.

Nelson reaches out, able to get a handful of hair. Heaves with all his might and Angelou slides over onto Nelson's trigger-foot.

Nelson ensures Angelou's bulk is on the IED, steps away. Angelou's weight takes, and Nelson snarls. "This is all your fault, fatty."

Angelou looks betrayed beyond all comprehension. His leg on fire, his soul empty. He openly cries as Nelson walks off. Nelson does not look back.

***

Nelson gets to the road, heads south maybe five hundred yards when he hears the IED *boom*.

***

Nelson could just spit, he was is so full of rage.

That girl. That freak hippie broad with her mysterious eco-terrorist and their ridiculous names and Angelou being such an inbred mother fucker all making trouble for a simple man in a world that shit the bed long ago and-

Nelson turns onto his property. The barn and stable sit a hundred yards in. south of that, another hundred yards, his farm house. And at the stable, a squirrely-looking doper. Just some average white kid who never ate meat and worshiped ideals that would only work in an ant colony.

Revolution, standing just outside the stable's fence, reeling in a bundle of chicken wire from the crowd of uncorked squirters. Revolution had actually fashioned some form of hook and line, cast it into the sea of the dead wandering about in the stable, snatched his girl's makeshift cage and was retrieving her. Towing that catch onto

100

the deck, as it were. How he pulled her off the stake was a question in and of itself.

But Henna was freed of it, being drug through the stable.

Nelson gawks, unable to comprehend the ludicrous turn of events. Just twenty-four hours ago he was as he had always been; a man surviving because he knew how to survive. And now, his last scavenger delivering him a plague. All Nelson had asked for was to be given something new and exciting. He got this.

"I will fucking kill you!" He draws his revolver and charges.

Revolution heaves one last time and Henna is drug to the stable fence. At the gate. Revolution swings it open, drags Henna through and shoves it shut as squirters meander up to it. The gate's lower corner plows a line through the dirt, roughing up a mound. Revolution can't get it shut all the way and sees Nelson gaining ground.

Shots fired.

Nelson knows he only has five rounds left after shooting Angelou. The first two bullets go wild; somewhere in the backdrop a brown, crinkly leaf clinging to an autumn tree branch for dear life suffers Nelson's rage as a bullet punches a hole through it.

Shoots again, this time with about thirty yards between them. Revolution takes the hit and spins. Fresh blood peppers the squirters just on the other side of the fence. They screech into a frenzy. That taste, that delicious, life-giving taste. It has returned.

The squirters mindlessly walk into the fence. They bounce back, walk a little harder into it a second time. Then a third. Fourth. All of them. Some hitting the gate, foam burbling over. Torrents.

Revolution's shoulder screams bloody murder. His foot still wedged against the gate to stem the tide of squirters. His hands are torn to shreds, wrestling open the chicken wire wrap. Henna fights and struggles with him. The wrap opens and she hurries to sit up as Revolution stumbles. The gate un-wedges; Henna shoves her foot there in Revolution's place.

Squirters fall to their knees and try and bite though the gap. Nelson slows to a trot and smiles. Beams. Exuberant. One round left. Revolution hit. Henna freed of her cocoon but it tangles around her. Her own foot keeping their death at bay while the squirters try and gnaw on her.

Revolution looks over Nelson's shoulder, reaches into his jacket. Pulls out a gun he's owned since the apocalypse occurred. He fired it dry a year ago but has used it on two occasions throughout the years as a bluff against other survivors. No one wants to get shot, but no one *really* wants to get shot with no hospital around. Ever again.

Revolution points the weapon. Henna looks up, sees how there is no magazine seated in the pistol grip. Just a gapping, empty hole. Like Nelson's compassion. She and Revolution make eye contact. Nervous. No good way out.

Teeth still gnaw near her foot. They're getting closer.

Nelson sees the semi-auto Revolution draws. Nelson slows up. Takes several calming breaths. His aim is terrible this far out; the one shot he landed on Revolution was a lucky one. He hoped he didn't use all his good fortune to just wing the punk.

Nelson stops. Steadies himself. He won't let his entire world crumble just because Angelou kidnapped some broad as an offering. With Angelou dead, he might as well get out of the squirter business. Just ration through the winter, then farm like a mother fucker for his remaining years.

Nelson adopts a shooting stance. Steadies the gun. Breathe in through the nose, out through the mouth. Shoot the dude. Henna will either keep her foot on the gate and let Nelson get his hands on her, or she'll try and run. In which case, the squirters, now in their feeding frenzy, they'll get loose.

She won't make it. Nelson will hightail it to the house where his armory is. Various hunting rifles and two more shotguns at the ready. Not set up for combat like his sawed-off, but with the refuge of four walls and a second floor elevation, the squirters will be easy pickings.

Nelson closes his left eye, lines his right one up on the sights. Savors this.

***

The pain is excruciating and he is nearly dead, but all that matters now is he rolled away fast enough to miss the full brunt of the blast.

Thank God for explosives built by amateurs. It went off, but the delay was just enough. Just enough.

Sure, Angelou's body is shredded on the outside and probably bleeding out inside. No doubt he had ruptures everywhere. His leg is a grizzled mess, but a thick branch near to him is an acceptable crutch for five hundred yards. Revenge is a wonderful fuel supply. It makes the agony take a back seat to purpose.

Hurriedly, reassembled the sawed-off. He found one shell.

Angelou could swear that dirty hippie queef saw him over Nelson's shoulder, but oh well. Angelou will be dead in moments anyways. He can feel the tongue of the Grim Reaper licking up his neck.

Angelou levels the sawed-off, and with one sudden *boom* lays at least six of the buck shot pellets into the back of Nelson's legs.

***

"HOLY FUCKING DOG SHIT OH MY GOD OHMYFUCKINGGOD!"

Nelson's legs pepper with explosions of pain. Knees buckle. Lined-up shot goes haywire; punctures the sky. He drops, spins around. Sees yet another unbelievable sight.

Revolution seizes the moment. Grabs Henna. Tows her up and they start to move. The gate swings open and the real shit begins.

ACT III –

Run. The world has gone to shit thanks to sexual

Deviants and a pair of smelly hippie queefs

Their eyes looks so much different now that he is defenseless against them.

Nelson can see out of the corner of his eye as both hippies stumble, holding on to one another. Revolution is losing blood. Henna looks like her ankle is broken after holding the door with her foot. Those squirters were hitting it pretty hard by the end. Together they yank on each other, one taking a step forward while the other stumbles, then vice versa. They'll die. In the end, they all do.

"Serves you right, you cunt!" Nelson shouts. He tries to ignore the pain his legs. He flexes them, tries to stand. Feels a few pellets shift under his flesh. Incredible needles of pain. Grits his teeth. Finger reflexively yanks the trigger, hears the empty *click click click* as the cylinder rotates spent casing after spent casing.

Nelson looks back, sees Angelou grinning. "Fuck you Angelou! Fuck you! This is all your fault!"

Angelou titters, looks satisified as his blubber, all chewed to fuck by the explosion, it just jiggles a little here and there. "You happy now? How's this for happy you fat cocksucker?"

And nelson whistles that high, shrill ululating note. Angelou's face drops. He knows that sound.

***

Angelou stares as the pits arrive and Nelson points towards him.

"*Kill*," Nelson says. Nelson claws at the ground and gets on his feet just as the squirters get to him. The dogs burst through, and look so hungry from all their forced starvation that Angelou wishes he had picked up a second shotgun shell.

For himself.

***

Nelson starts a jagged run/stumble away from the herd of squirters when the tattooed one breaks through, jaw slung so low it's like she dislocated it.

Angelou's horrifying screams echo through the farm. Nelson stumbles backwards and the squirter drops to her knees beside him. Nelson can hear the foam froth up in her mouth, bulging out from between her teeth like someone lit off a fire extinguisher in her throat.

Angelou on his back like a turtle, arms and legs thrashing helplessly as everything around him drops down to take a bite. Wet rending sounds and gurgling. Spasms, gushing. One squirter backs away, a slippery length of intestine captured in her clenching, rabid jaw. She lumbers backwards and it keeps coming and coming and coming and coming and coming…

Nelson kicks at the foaming squirter's face. Breaks her nose; cocks it off to the side at a hideous angle. No blood, no swelling. He kicks again. Her head snaps back. Foam falls off in clumps. She nearly topples backwards but flexes forward hard. Comes again.

Nelson kicks a third time, misses. His leg lands over her shoulder and she goes for it. He scissors her with his other leg, distress charging up and down his legs as the buckshot wounds sizzle his nerves.

He yanks hard but he doesn't know what he's doing. No formal training, here, ladies and gentlemen. Just heave-ho enough and that sound do it, right? The squirter's head turns. Some. That's all. She snarls. Nelson tries to whistle for the dogs but they're over with the other squirters, everybody eating Angelou. Foam everywhere like it was snowing. The squirters foam so much more when they devour. The dogs don't mind. People taste good.

Nelson kicks the squirter again. Jumps to his feet. Legs shrieking bloody murder but he stays up. Jumps up like he's a rock star doing a dive off stage, lands with both feet plowing into the squirter's neck and face.

Bones crunch. Her skin tears with an unzipping sound. He jumps two more times until he sees brain fly out. He falls back again. Tries to catch his breath. Relief floods him, counteracting the adrenaline.

Two of the squirters look up from Angelou's gelatinous corpse, clumps of grisly flab dangling comically. Eyeball Nelson. Start coming over.

On his feet, nelson knows he has to run until he collapses inside. Hole up. He turns away from the sight. The squirters, one an old woman who was missing an eye after Dennis had a round with her. The other a small girl. Both soaked in blood and fat chunks.

Nelson run/stumbles as fast as he can. His bowels quiver. He wants to piss himself. He wants to fall into a ball and make it all go away. He wants a gun. But he settles for the new wash of intoxicating adrenaline tickling his every fiber.

The house seems so far. An eternity. But the hidden camera room where the scavengers play with the squirters…that is around the corner. There's the shotgun loaded to bear against a freed zombie-

"Jackpot!" Nelson exclaims. Beaming, Exuberant. Runs around the corner.

Runs into Revolution, a wood cutting axe over his head. Already swinging down.

***

Revolution swings one-handed; his other arm dangles lifelessly at his side.

The dude is pale. So is Henna. Revolution's blood is everywhere but inside his veins. The axe comes down and Nelson dodges, blocks, takes the blade along his ribcage.

Nelson roars and feels his heart triple in speed. *Not now.* Revolution does his best to wind up for another one and swings but Nelson throws a horrible karate chop and deflects it. The handle catches Nelson's forearm. Something in there breaks.

Nelson skids, tackles Revolution. The hippie gives easy. This is obviously his last stand. He knows he's going to die. He's bled out. Nelson punches him once and gets no resistance. Stands. Grabs the axe.

"I blame you for this also. Just so you know." And Nelson swings the axe into Revolution's chest.

"No!" Henna screams, lurches and sways on her feet. Nelson backhands her and she falls near the storm cellar door. She cries, rolls over.

Nelson turns back to Revolution, smiles. Feral. "I'll take this." And he grips the axe handle, heaves. Revolution flops with the effort, drops back to the ground when the axe head comes free.

Nelson starts to walk away, then turns around and swings again. And again. And again. Another time and the axe head breaks off the handle, cheap as it is.

Out of breath, Nelson looks at the bludgeoned dude—a kid, really, despite his life as a terrorist—and is impressed by how much blood in this pale kid still managed to spray out as the axe did its worst. Nelson can taste it. Panics for a brief second and hopes beyond hope Revolution wasn't infected.

That fear is broken, though, as the pits appear around the same corner Nelson just rounded. But the pits, they're not looking so hot.

"Your dogs look infected there," Henna sobs, but her voice the peaceful sound of resignation. "Can animals get-"

Typhoid Mary Zombie. Here. In my stable. Nelson doesn't care. He realizes it and it's too late now.

He grabs Henna as the dogs start off at a dead sprint. Nelson swings open the storm cellar door, shoves her down. Jumps into it himself, swings the door closed as a muzzle breaks the barrier and snaps. Nelson yanks on the door with all his might, but the pit gets its head inside.

***

A battle of epic proportions.

The storm cellar was like all storm cellars: a burrow dug in the earth for families to take shelter in when tornadoes kick up. Dark, claustrophobic. Doors at a hefty angle nearly level with the ground.

Nelson, both hands white-knuckling the door handle, his feet planted so firm against the lip of the stairs going in, straining hard enough to squeeze out the buckshot pellets, back and chest flexing like they're trying to break out of his clothes, head thrown back, teeth grinding. Lips peeled away, trembling.

One of the pits he'd abused and neglected its whole life, trained to be obedient for fear of retaliation, prodded into ferocity, now as undead as everything else in the world. Scrambling against the metal door. Claws raking the outside. Body flailing. Head wedged inside. Jaws snapping. Eyes as desolate as scrubland, still fixated on Nelson's throat.

"Just stop fighting," Henna says, rising to a sitting position. Hands on her belly, she considers the shadows draped over her and knows those dark veils are just the first harbingers of their doom.

"How about you get up here and help me?"

"I want to die."

"I'm going to keep you alive for a long time, little missy. *That* you can-" the pit snaps hungrily, eager to return a favor or two to Nelson. Nelson yanks the door and risks hammer-punching the dog in the flat of its head. "*That,* little missy, you can take to the bank."

"No banks left."

108

"Weeks! I said weeks!" Nelson says. He raises another fist and the pit follows it, ready to latch on this time.

Instead, Nelson throws a knee, a bizarre upper cut that whacks the dog's head backwards and out of the door. Hard. It whines in a pathetic puppy tone as Nelson gives everything he has and slams the door shut. Throws the bolt.

Lets himself fall back, lands hard. Sits against the dank wall, alone in the darkness despite the fact Henna is so close her body heat reaches him.

His side burns inexorably from the axe wound. His forearm makes its deep bone wound known now that he isn't wrenching on the door. His legs ach like they had been hammered. Stung. A million wasps under his flesh, writhing and striking.

His throat raw, his heart struggling to downshift. His mind overwhelmed, his eyes, sore. His life, sore. His future…unknown now.

He can hear Henna breathing; even in the dark he can see her holding her belly. Her skin pale, nearly glowing in the umber.

Too tired. Exhausted doesn't fit the bill. Bankrupt. Enfeebled even. His eyelids weigh like anchors. All he wanted to do was collapse under the pressure of sleep. "Weeks, little missy." He says, even his words tuckered out.

"Okay," Henna says, closes her eyes. Gone.

"Weeks…" and Nelson's eyes close on the sight of Henna's belly, and his mind drifts off on the thought of what he was going to do to that baby when he just had the strength.

All those things…

***

Nelson comes to, and his body tells him it has been hours, days, weeks now.

The dark in the cellar, so dingy and consuming he doesn't know what is what anymore. His eyes work to adjust to the slight bleed of what might be dawn seeping in through the cellar door's rickety frame.

Sitting up, he can feel that he wet his pants in the night. It got everywhere, sitting in a pool of it. Stunk like all the sour fragrances of life that people never knew existed until they smelled them. Piss, shit, blood, guts, rot, decay, damp earth, failure, hurt, dreams left in messy ribbons, cut and strewn about.

Al he wanted to do was whore out the undead and make a goddamn honest living in this aftermath. "Fuck me," Nelson laments.

Moves his hands, feels the tacky texture of the pool of urine he lays in-

Tacky.

Tacky.

Lifts his hand to his nose, smells his fingers. Copper. Not brine. Copper.

Nelson looks to Henna. She stares lifelessly at him, listless as a corpse should be. Her right eye hollow. A gaping crevice. Her left eye, possessed and hideous like any squirter. Her mouth, dried foam crusting down her lips onto her torn-out throat.

Nelson sits frozen, smells his own feces as he evacuates himself.

Limping like she broke her ankle holding the gate. Some of them were hitting it pretty hard

Not broken. Bit. Gotten by a squirter.

She died while he slept, turned. Eaten. By what? They don't eat themselves. They don't-

Things change. Mutation. Now it jumps from species to species and-

Her belly. Flat. Her groin, punched out from the inside in a repugnant wreck of flesh and blood.

Nelson looks down, sees a little something at the stump of his foot—fresh and gleaming in the new day's ambiance—a little something gumming its way up his leg.

That little something, it's trailing an umbilical cord.

ABOUT THE AUTHORS

Ryan Sayles is Midwestern and prior military. A post-September 11th world got him into assigned to an anti-terrorism unit where he spent five years staring at dark waters and waiting for dirty bombs that thankfully never arrived.

His fiction has been included in two print anthologies; one by the now apparently defunct Short Story Library and the Editors & Preeditors nominated horror site SNM Horror Mag. More of his stuff has been displayed at Shotgun Honey, Nefarious Muse and The Flash Fiction Offensive.

He has a novel out from Snubnose Press entitled "The Subtle Art of Brutality", set in the fictional city of Saint Ansgar and follows the exploits of former homicide detective-turned private investigator Richard Dean Buckner. Stories about him have been published at Shotgun Honey and, under the pen name Derek Kelly, at Crime Factory and Beat to a Pulp.

***

Brian Panowich is a Southern Gentleman clearly riding Ryan's coattails. You can find all the stuff he has floating in the ether at www.amazon.com/Brian-Panowich and at Panowich.com. And his wife's name really is Dawn.

HEY, THAT ROBOT ATE MY BABY! Volume 1.

6 Mind-bending Science Fiction tales to astonish and offend...

Featuring:

Timejacked: The Rand Paradox
By Chuck Regan
In the 24th Century, the ultimate form of vanity is to create a personal alternate Earth timeline. Chlör Byzantine, a B-Grade web celebrity, travels to 1957 to stop Ayn Rand from ruining the future... but she is ready and waiting for him.

The Whores of God
By Chris Leek
Earth in the 22nd Centaury is a nice place to visit, but you wouldn't want to live there; the moral majority has taken a stand and if you want your kicks in 2132 you have to go off-world to get them. In the international waters of deep space everything is available, for a price. Jensen Corduroy is on a mission to get laid, but the Reverend Ellroy has a much higher purpose, he is on a mission from God.

This Protean Love
By Isaac Kirkman
Adelita Salazar, the last living border agent of her precinct patrols the Tierras Oscuras, the Dark Lands, in search of her missing brother, encountering killers, and refugees, human, and machine in a futuristic world where the nature of reality is as uncertain as her future.

Hack Job, Inc.
By Rich Osburn
In the year 2092, New Bangkok is a teeming mass of over 35 million people above ground. Among them is Takei Miushito, a tattoo artist versed in neuro-ink, an ink infused with neurological source coding designed to hack the human mind, triggering a state of euphoria. But times are tough, so when she is approached with life changing money to infuse altered source code, she can't pass it up – until her clients begin turning up dead.

Wherever The Light Ends
By Ryan Sayles
In 1947, twins sisters disappear from the face of the Earth during the most horrific experience of their lives. Later they are found, and they have new parents, new scars and a desire for a new life. When they die in 2012, shut-ins and with no family and no friends, the results of that one disappearance mark the end for mankind.

Geek Squad 2.0
By Brian Panowich
In the 60's and 70's they did it with a bullet. In the 80's and 90's they did it with the media, but today if you want someone dead, it's as easy as a Google search. The Geek Squad, bringing assassination to the modern age, but still can't get dates for the prom.

HAMMER DOWN

www.ingramcontent.com/pod-product-compliance
Lightning Source LLC
Chambersburg PA
CBHW030552130626
46552CB00006B/2522